Red Deer
PRESS

mOsH Pit

KristYn duNniOn

published by

Red Deer Press
813 MacKimmie Library Tower
2500 University Drive N.W.
Calgary Alberta Canada T2N 1N4
www.reddeerpress.com

credits

Edited for the Press by Peter Carver
Copyedit by Jacqui Swedberg
Cover and text design by Erin Woodward
Cover photo by Shawn Smith. Lily Suicide appears courtesy of
SuicideGirls.com. Background image courtesy Milena, self-portrait
Printed and bound in Canada by Friesens for Red Deer Press

acknowledgments

Financial support provided by the Canada Council, the Department of
Canadian Heritage, the Alberta Foundation for the Arts, a beneficiary of the
Lottery Fund of the Government of Alberta, and the University of Calgary.

THE CANADA COUNCIL | LE CONSEIL DES ARTS
FOR THE ARTS | DU CANADA
SINCE 1957 | DEPUIS 1957

National Library of Canada
Cataloguing in Publication

Dunnion, Kristyn, 1969–
Mosh pit / Kristyn Dunnion.
ISBN 0-88995-292-2
I. Title.
PS8557.U552M68 2004   jC813'.6   C2004-904895-3

5 4 3 2 1

For punkers everywhere, with love.

Acknowledgements

Very special thanks to my editor and mentor, Peter Carver, without whom none of this would be possible. Fond thanks go to my writing group, comrades and cohorts all, and especially to Carolyn Beck, Hilary Cameron, Lena Coakley, Rosemary Hood, Joellen Housego, and Kathy Stinson, who read earlier drafts of this work and gave invaluable feedback and encouragement. Thanks to Julian Calleros for Spanish consultation; any remaining errors are my own! I borrowed "scab-faced hoor" from the generous and debonair Darrin Currell. Cheers to CBC's Brave New Waves and Nightlines for saving my isolated, alienated teenage soul. Lastly, I am extremely grateful for Milena Soczka's steadfast patience and her good humor, and for my parents' continued love and support.

Contents

Book One: Cherry's Prom

Chapter 1: In the Beginning 12

Chapter 2: Cherry's High School Send-off 19

Chapter 3: Primping 23

Chapter 4: Clubbing 28

Chapter 5: Satan's Playhouse 31

Chapter 6: Exit Light 38

Chapter 7: Escape from Satan's Playhouse 42

Chapter 8: Chillin' 44

Chapter 9: Now What? 51

Chapter 10: After Hours 57

Chapter 11: Cherry's Place 63

Book Two: Spiraling

Chapter 12: Fountain of Youth   78

Chapter 13: Our New Job   89

Chapter 14: Going Home   101

Chapter 15: The Tomb   111

Chapter 16: Man-To-Man   116

Chapter 17: *La Cena con Carlotta y Su Familia*   125

Chapter 18: Sexy Carol   135

Chapter 19: So, Suddenly It Was A Date!   141

Chapter 20: Tom Boy Meets Aphrodite   145

Chapter 21: Payback   156

Chapter 22: Amnesia   159

Chapter 23: Comatose   166

Chapter 24: Exam   168

Book Three: Revelations

Chapter 25: Cherry Pushed Me   178

Chapter 26: Hey, Vincent!   186

Chapter 27: Lazy Afternoon   191

Chapter 28: Score!   199

Chapter 29: Dime Store   202

Chapter 30: No Show   207

Chapter 31: Cassandra   212

Chapter 32: Labyrinth   216

Chapter 33: Velvetine and Diesel   219

Chapter 34: Calling Cherry   229

Chapter 35: Ambush at Punker Park   234

Chapter 36: Resistance is Fertile   242

Chapter 37: Rescue Squad   250

Chapter 38: Bail Court   255

Chapter 39: Mosh Pit Revisited   261

Chapter 40: Into the Sunset   267

book one:

CHeRRy's PrOM

chapter one:
In the Beginning

In the beginning, there was Cherry and me.

Now there isn't.

The story I'm trying to tell you is about all the stuff in between.

It all started the night of Cherry's Prom. The day she dropped out of high school. That's when she fell in love. That's the night Cherry started blossoming into the hideous, weedy monster I grew to hate.

But I'm getting a bit ahead of myself. I better go back to that same afternoon in May, back to the girls' bathroom at our high school.

Mr. Merrick had been hassling Cherry in geography class, about not doing her homework and not paying attention and for having a bad attitude in general, or something, and Cherry told Mr. Merrick to go fuck himself and she walked right out. Out the door, down the hall, straight to the bathroom and lit up a joint. She inhaled deeply, leaned against the sink, and said she was dropping out. I wasn't there, but I heard all about it soon enough. In a way I don't know what the big deal was. It's not like she *enjoyed* school or was any good at it. She would rather party all night and sleep all day than go to school. She said she'd even rather work all day, *even* at the checkout over at the American Whoremart. She'd rather make some money and spend it all than go to school. It was the place where we hung out until we were old enough to hang out somewhere better. Now she was seventeen and her mother didn't give a shit what she did, so long as it wasn't in her or her ugly new boyfriend's way.

Later, up on the roof of Cherry's building I tried to talk her out of it.

"Merry Dick says I missed more classes than I actually went to," she said. "And I never handed in that stoopid essay."

"So?" I said. Not much of a motivational speech.

"Well, what's the point? Even if I get, like, perfect on the final he'll still fail me. My other classes are just as bad."

"Hmm." I peeked at her out the corner of my eye. This was obviously bugging her. I mean nobody likes to fail. But it wasn't a huge surprise, really.

"Merrick said I was a colossal waste of space, a piece of trash, and I'd never amount to anything."

I said, "Whoa. He doesn't even know you. He has no business saying shit like that. It's just 'cause he's scared of you, that's all."

We sat there quietly for a bit, me thinking what kind of insecure dork Mr. Merrick was to say something so mean, and Cherry? . . . well, I had no idea what Cherry was thinking. Hopefully not about those words that branded their way through her.

"What about summer school?" I said. "Then you can make up the rest next year, and you won't have to have that prick for a teacher again."

"Naw. Summer school sucks."

She had me there.

"Fuck it," she said. "I'm getting a job."

"Well," I said after a bit. "I'll really miss you, Cherry." Because I couldn't imagine school without her. . . I couldn't imagine anything without her, back then.

Cherry laughed and snorted, and I kept saying what's so funny, you know, but finally she got it together and said, "Duh, Simone, you're coming with me."

"Maybe," I said. I smoked a cigarette.

I thought about it and although my track record wasn't as bad as hers, there was no love lost between me and most of my teachers. Except Ms. Flores. She taught French and had great legs and always wore tight, short skirts that held my interest. I had unlimited fantasies about her keeping me after school and teaching me manners, but no such luck.

C'est la vie, cherie.

I'm not dumb. Not like everyone thinks, anyway. Some people—like almost every single adult, for example—as soon as they even see me, they expect me to be stupid. But that's because they don't like the way I dress and they hate my hair. Being a dyke doesn't help matters, either. Adults automatically think I have some kind of authority problem, which I very well may have, but I still don't think you should assume that everyone with a big sick Mohawk has a problem, and everyone with nice, curly blonde hair doesn't.

In fact, I'd always been pretty quiet at school. If I went to class and stayed awake, I did okay. I even liked it. I thought about Carlotta and Pretty Boi and Sexy Carol, about how hard they worked to do well, and how they all had ideas and dreams for after purgatory. They'd always been more self-motivated, as the guidance counselors like to say. They hated authority at least as much as us, but they had learned the hard way to avoid conflict, to fly under the radar, to not rattle the cages of those administrative wieners. They acted like there was more to look forward to after this incarceration. Like it was temporary. Back then I didn't understand that, and Cherry even less than me. To us, high school was a shipwreck; we fought exhaustion in infinite waters, hung our heavy limbs in an eternal dead man's float, world without end, amen.

I thought about my mother. Not that she'd really notice if I dropped out or anything, but if she *could* comprehend the situation, I'm sure she'd forbid it the way a normal parent would.

I knew right then I wouldn't be dropping out. Cherry knew it, too, but we both pretended there was nothing about to change between us. We sparked up another joint and smoked, looking out over the city. The sky was getting dark and sirens wailed past and people were out, doing things. Windows were open to catch some air, radios played in different kitchens. Cars bumped and squealed down the ratty street and heavy hip hop bass lines filled your head, your chest, and made you think about things like dancing. Not going and doing homework and getting a good night's sleep and trotting off to school like some TV sitcom kid. It made you feel like dressing up and putting on makeup and sneaking into clubs and dancing all night long. It made you feel sexy and tough and dangerous and that's exactly what we were.

So that's exactly what we did.

On second thought, maybe I should back up and start at the very, very beginning.

The day Cherry picked me.

Grade seven, Memorial Public School, afternoon recess. Me, the new kid. Shy. Dorky. Wearing floods and secondhand running shoes, too big for my feet. Clothes they gave me at the women's shelter where me and my mom were staying while my mom had a little rest and got herself organized and looked for an apartment for us. I hadn't spoken a word all fall, not to anyone. The teacher was nice. Mrs. Bronson. She smelled like cake. She made me stay in for my first few days. While the other kids ran around screaming, and skipped rope, and played kissing tag, she smiled and fed me crackers and cheese from her own lunch box. She tried to coax me out of my shell. She said things like she knew I was having a hard time at home (*home?*) and I could always tell her anything that was bothering me, and that sort of thing.

I remember wanting more cheese and also not wanting to eat in front of her. I'd slide the pieces in my zip-up jacket and wait for her to finish. Then I'd take them to the girls' bathroom and sit on a toilet in the stall and eat, so I could turn around and spit out if I had to. Back then, food would sometimes fly right out of my mouth when I most wanted it to stay in.

I guess I was cramming them in, fastfast, when Cherry found me. She kicked the door of my stall and said it was hers, and that I had to get out and use a different one. I froze. She kicked and kicked and I was worried the door would fly open and send me reeling, but no. The door didn't reach all the way down to the floor so she lay down and slid under, into the cubicle. She stood up and towered over me. Her red hair was tangled and she had gray shadow smeared on her eyelids. It made her pale face look ghostly but her eyes sparkled with magic.

I was on the toilet, mouth full of crackers.

"You didn't shit, did you?" she asked.

I shook my head and tried to swallow those dry, tickly crumbs.

"Good. Get off." Cherry unzipped her pants and stepped right out of them. I couldn't breathe. She was wearing cotton bikini panties that said Tuesday in blue letters.

She pulled me up and took my spot, tugged down her underpants, and peed loudly into the bowl. She had a big bruise on the inside of one thigh.

"Whatcha staring at?" she said. She was very tough.

I nodded at her panties, dangling there, twisted so the cotton crotch of them turned up and out towards me. I could see a little damp mark she'd made there.

"Hey?" she barked at me.

"Today's Wednesday," I whispered.

Cherry stared hard at me. Then she started laughing. She laughed and laughed and said I was funny. She declared it out loud and so I was. No one ever thought that about me before. No one ever thought anything about me before. I *became* funny because she thought I was. I became.

"You're my friend, now. Okay?" she said.

It wasn't like a real question, though.

She never expected me to answer.

chapter two:
Cherry's High School Send Off

So. Me and Cherry got the boot from Cherry's mom 'coz she had a Date and we both said, "Whateve', we're outta here."

Cherry said, "Oh, by the way, I dropped out today," and her mom goes, "Good. Now you can get a job and make a little money. I'm sick of paying for you all the time," which is a total joke since she hardly pays for anything and can't wait for the baby bonus each month so she can get two cartons of smokes and some booze.

I still think Cherry wouldn't have done half the things she did if she wasn't always scrounging. Hungering for all those things we were and weren't supposed to have. More than clean clothes and three meals a day. Money and power and glamor and respect and love—the obliterating, feverish, addictive kind, that coursed through your veins and froze your heart.

Bam.

At Cherry's we could do practically whatever we wanted. So of course we were almost always there. If Cherry's mom was in a good mood she'd sit in the living room, smoking and laughing and pouring us drinks. She'd tell us stories about creepy guys who promise everything until you let them down your pants. Then they steal your bankcard, guess your PIN number, and leave you with a scorching case of herpes. She oughta know.

"Maybe you got the right idea, Simone," she'd say. "I never tried it with a Lesbo, but there was One once that used to send me love notes. Weird, huh?"

Me and Cherry laughed hysterically, one because we couldn't imagine her mom with a dyke, and two because I guess she didn't know half of what went on under her own roof.

But on the night of Cherry's high school send-off—Cherry's prom, we were calling it—we were sent packing. So no chin-wagging that night. Instead, we trucked on over to my mom's apartment to get ready. A definite second choice.

The Tomb is totally different. It's quiet. Clean. Plastic, vinyl, and retro linoleum.

The Tomb is a postcard for pharmaceutical success.

Leave it to Bi-Polar Beaver.

Mister Merry Dick the Prick put me over the edge. I am so serious. I totally hate him. I can't believe he ever found anyone stupid enough to marry him. His wife must be a fucking loser retard. He stands there with his hands shoved in his pockets, in the same ugly green pants every day of the week, every week of the year. The only thing different about them is his ass, which keeps getting fatter. How can he teach geography? What a joke! Mothahfuckah's never been on a plane in his life. I am so getting him back for the shit he said about me in front of the whole class. The only good thing is I finally quit school. Tuned in, Turned on, Dropped out! YAY. Cherry's Prom starts tonight at Satan's Playhouse for the Cuntagion show around eleven, then

I'm partying all night long, so whoever's not a loser ass can celebrate with me.

Mood: Pissed off and Pent up
Music: Lunachicks "Binge and Purge!"

chapter three:
Primping

"I look sooo hot!" Cherry stood in all her nude glory and blew a kiss to the mirror. "Check my new lipstick."

We were at The Tomb, in the antiseptic tiled bathroom. I was looking at Cherry in the mirror.

I said, "Took you long enough. Show starts at 11:00, you know."

But really, I was thinking, *she's right.* She was even more gorgeous than usual. Dark-rimmed eyes, big enough to burst, with deep smoky shadows around them, blinked back at me in the reflection. Her succulent, pouting lips were the exact same, deep red shine as her pigtails and her new, shoplifted PVC collar.

How could she be so casual about it, about this strange beauty? She was a demonic nymph, all bird bones and soft hairless skin, glittering here and there with sparkles and pieces of silver jewelry—rings on fingers, toes, labret, navel, nose. She reached over to sift through the pile of clothes we dragged into the locked bathroom and I soaked up her nakedness, trailed my eyes down that pale backside, thrilled at her dimpled bum and her long, bare legs.

"Now tie this fucker up," she said, chucking the thing right at me.

So I did. We hoisted the full-bodied, black, vintage corset on her, the one she had discovered at the bottom of some over-looked barrel at the secondhand clothing store down the street. I pulled and laced, and Cherry barked out orders and twisted to try and get a good look in the mirror at the same time.

"Tighter, for fuck's sake," she yelled. "I want cleavage, for once."

"You can have mine," I mumbled.

"Shut up, Simone. You have great tits and you don't even know how to use them. It's a crime," she said, for the millionth time.

My cheeks burned and I hunched forward, thinking *if they're so great why don't you do something with them?!* But instead I said, "Smells like mothballs, Cherr. Sure you don't want to wash it first? Or air it out or something?"

She lit up a smoke and told me to fuck off.

"Cherry, don't smoke in here. My mom will probably call the cops on us again," I hissed.

"Maybe they'll lock her up for good this time and we can totally party here."

24

I grabbed the cigarette and flushed it, sprayed air freshener around, and slapped her butt for good measure.

"Behave," I said. "Or I won't finish doing up this torture device."

Cherry said, "Whateve," and I did the final big tugs and loopy knots, and then Her Majesty took two weirdish looking foamy things and stuffed them right into the sagging pointy tips of the boob part of her corset.

"What?"

"Nothing." She rammed them in, one on each side and tried to plump the fabric out evenly.

"Cherry? Have you gone completely mental?" I said.

"Shut up. Your mom won't ever notice I borrowed them. For real!"

I knew my mother would never see those retro '80s detachable shoulder pads again. I could guarantee it.

"What's so funny?" Cherry snarled defensively. "They don't grow like they did, you know. Back in the fifties or whatever, like, everyone had pointy things. Not any more."

"Is that scientifically proven?" I asked, laughing.

"DUH," she said. She grabbed my green hair and rubbed the wood glue paste mixture into the roots, roughly. "It's from all those hormones in the meat! I read it somewhere."

"Gross. So glad I'm vegetarian," I said. "Ow, Cherry, that hurts."

"Just the price you pay for a beautiful Mohawk." Once the goop got worked in evenly from the roots to the tips, I'd hang at the waist and she'd blast my head with the hair dryer, pulling the ends to straighten and stiffen them, while the glue dried. Bent over like that usually left me hanging with Cherry's naked crotch inches from my face.

"I need a smoke," she yelled, over the roar of the dryer. And, "When are you gonna learn to do your own hair?"

The sudden silence, when she snapped off the machine and tossed it into the corner, deafened. I hair-sprayed and touched up the little flaccid pieces, and Cherry rolled on a sparkly Sacred Heart thong. Then she clipped her shredded fishnet stockings to the garters on her outfit.

A knock at the door made me jump. "Girls? Girls, are you in there?" My mother's voice wavered, all halting upward inflections.

"NO!" we yelled, on cue.

"You're not smoking in there, are you, girls?" she persisted.

I yelled, "No," and Cherry yelled, "Yes."

"Shit, Simone. You should've changed first," said Cherry.

I said, "I'm wearing this," pointing to my faded Joan Jett T-shirt and my über-patched, black combat pants.

"Wrong. You're whoring off your nice tits and ass or else we might not get into the fucking club, Simone."

"Shut up—she might hear you." Ironically, she'd be upset by the swearing, but not by where we were going or what we might do there. "Besides, I don't feel like getting all dressed up," I said. "We can always go around back and ask for Velvetine."

"Once we get those IDs off Hardcore Hank it won't matter, but until then you can make a little effort. You just want an excuse to hang out with those dykes in the band." Cherry yanked my belt and ripped open my fly, bit me hard on the neck, and smashed our chests together.

26

"Easy with those weapons." I laughed. She wouldn't stop bomping my boobs, or ripping off my clothes, and we were both laughing hysterically.

My mom kept knocking on the bathroom door and hissing, "Girls? Girls, what's going on in there? What is so darn funny?"

I could see my mother's face, as though the door was made of glass, not wood. Worried brows, slightly unfocused eyes, small pursed lips, underneath a careful pile of ash-blonde curls. I felt a pang of remorse and pushed Cherry away.

Cherry threw our identical bondage kilts up in the air. One landed in the sink, the other dangerously close to the toilet. She was still laughing, but I was quieting down, thinking of the distracted, vulnerable woman pacing the plastic carpet covering in the hall. I slipped out, closed the door behind me, and took my mom to the kitchen for tea while Cherry finished her fashion-based tactical maneuvers and sipped bourbon from her silver flask.

Thirty minutes later, we were both dolled up beyond recognition. Huge polished boots gleamed up to our fishnetted knees and postage stamp skirts fluttered over our bums when we raced out the door, grabbing our jackets on the way.

And so began the fated night of Cherry's high school send-off: Cherry's Prom.

chapter four

Clubbing

"Let' s see some ID, sweethearts."

A mountain of manhood blocked the inner hallway. Music pounded around him, from all the corners he didn't take up.

Cherry stepped close to him and said, "You don't know my birthday?"

I smiled and Cherry swung her kilt and his eyes narrowed, so we smiled more. My lips were stretched tight, pulled back behind my ears. Cherry twirled a pigtail with her finger. His face relaxed a smidgen. His eyelids rolled down halfway. He shifted his weight slightly, so all the important parts pushed toward us more.

"So . . . uh . . . when is it?" He licked his lips.

"Next week," she said. "Will you remember me and my girlfriend? Say, with a nice cocktail?" She enunciated crisply. Even though I wanted to puke I winked at him.

"What day?" I could see his throat working. He was thinking "girlfriend" like the kind in the porno videos, the girlfriends that always need a big man like him to help them out. He measured us all over with his eyes, didn't try to hide it. I imagined him checking our molars, tapping them for weak spots and cavities. Cherry placed her cool hand on his hairy forearm and leaned in closer. Her corset points jabbed lightly into his abdomen.

"Thursday," she whispered, all husky.

We brushed past and I let my eyes linger on his face, all haughty, then lowered them and opened my lips slightly.

This was the most important moment, because if you act sexy *and* superior you can usually pull it off without actually having to pull, if you know what I mean. With most guys, that is, unless they're super arrogant, woman-hating bastards. If you do it just right, letting them *think* about it is enough. If you get the wrong combination of sexy and insecure, then they think you're a tinny slut and call your bluff and you'd end up in the back like some girls we knew, doing stuff for real to get what we got for nothing.

That would not be good.

The other thing: guys apparently really go for the slightly open mouth trick. That's what Cherry always said, and she oughtta know. Cherry's the Scam Queen. I just tagged along and played off the sparks. So it helps if you're wearing lip gloss. But, if you don't have any of that, you can hork up some spittle and slowly lick your lips to coat them. You can bite your bottom lip and pout a bit or, if you have a lollipop, you give it a good suck. That really works. Then as you're walking away, after you get in free or get your drink or whatever, it's very important to sway your hips. That's the icing on the cake.

You want to leave them with that warm, tingly sensation that you're a real sex-bomb and aren't they so lucky to have had this little encounter, and geez, maybe she really likes me, and I guess I'm quite a stud after all!

That way they'll do it again next time. For you or for some other girl.

You, or she, might not even have to work so hard.

chapter five

Satan's Playhouse

Inside Satan's Playhouse I dropped the feminine wiles crap. The place was packed. Music raged mega decibels, shook bodies around the smoky, dark room. I rolled up the sleeves of my customized jean jacket to reveal rows of spikes on my leather gauntlets. Cherry took off and tried to score. I cruised around a bit before circling back to get a beer at the bar. It was hard to see through the dry ice and pulsing lights, but I knew my friends were there someplace. Carlotta and Pretty Boi and Gorgeous Carol maybe, Velvetine and Hardcore Hank.

That night there was an odd mix of hard-core punks, some Goths looking drastic in pancake makeup and black spidery clothes, and lots of metal heads. There was a busload of suburban kids, thanks to a so-called alternative radio station that overplayed one crap song by the headliners. Some whiny emo boy band. All soft cock compared to the local legendary metal chicks in Cuntagion.

I lit up a smoke and stood apart from the crowd to get a good gander at the stage. Now more than ever I wished I could play well, wished I could be a part of this scene, rocking hard with a band like them. Choosy Soozy, the lead singer, was jumping around in a red, fun fur bikini top and low-slung, skintight, leopard print pants. Her platform boots had orangey red flames painted up to the knee. She shook her long, bleached hair and vocally assaulted the crowd. Low growls built to operatic intensity; her voice spanned octaves.

To her left was Velvetine's girlfriend, Diesel. She hammered away on the bass, fingers blurred in motion. Her arms were probably as big as the bouncer's. She moved around the stage, carnivorous, predatory. I hurt inside, soaking up her raw, alien beauty. My organs twisted and ached watching her. My stomach parts and even lower. I could barely see Snatch, the drummer, at the back of the stage behind the flames. Hatchet stopped her guitar riff long enough to breathe another mushroom cloud of fire up into the ceiling, inches above the ecstatic and singed crowd. Velvetine looked amazing! She was crawling around the stage dressed in a rubber nun's habit, dipping her neon rosary into people's drinks and sucking on the beads. Cuntagion kicked ass!

Partway into their set, I noticed Cherry in the middle of the pit, slamming and sweating away to the onslaught of drums and guitars. Every now and then I'd see her ripped leather vest with the giant glittery cherries on the back, before it melded with the rest of the punx. I pushed my way into the pit, got shoved into a mass of bone and leather, caught a glimpse of her, then lost it. The heat from all those thrashing bodies washed over me and I pogoed around, taking hits on all sides—not in a bad way, mind. A crash and a body check in there was like a smile and a handshake at the office water-cooler for other people. If you fell, someone pulled you back up. If you went flying too far back into the rows of people behind the pit, the standing-around-and-rocking-out-but-not-moshing people, they'd just give you a little push, back into the fray. Mosh pit etiquette, like.

So one more body check and I landed almost beside Cherry. She was yelling out the lyrics like everyone else. My adrenaline soared with the screaming guitars and I slammed into her. She grabbed me in a bear hug and lifted me up, up. The bottle I had went flying. We worked our way to the stage, taking out everyone on the way. Deep in the pit I felt no pain. The music was so loud up there by the speakers, it beat through our chests, moved blood to its rhythm. Music sand-blasted its way through all those layers of anger, confusion, frustration; it blew the hate right out of you, stripped you of all your petty failures, the endless disappointments and hurts that choked you the rest of your waking hours. Amid the bar-rage of body parts, in the steaming heat and noise, I offered up my body, my soul, to punkrawk salvation.

Cherry and I linked arms so we wouldn't be ripped apart by the guys all around us, twice our height and weight. We

33

were small but tough, and we loved to rock the pit. The few other girls in the pit homed in on our vibe and soon we were all one girl body, claiming a place in that madhouse and cutting loose the way we were meant to. Most guys backed off a bit and did their own thing. A couple of them were freaking out on way too much PCP, and the drug had hardened them, robotic. They tore up the place, hell-bent on violence, anger stiffening their muscles like lactic acid. They smashed in on us, all elbows and big boots, striking the soft spots we couldn't armor. Together, all us girls picked them out, one then the other, and heaved them onto the concrete floor, littered with broken bottles and beer. Cherry kicked the biggest one in the head until he left us alone to go and fight with his ugly friend. With them gone it was pure madness. Chicks ruled the pit, sweaty and euphoric. It was an estrogen invasion in the typically male-dominated underworld, and we fucking loved it.

At the end of the set, I hugged Cherry, laughing, and she hopped up, clamped her legs around my waist and smooched me, all over my face. I staggered under her slight weight, then braced myself, willed my quads to iron. Soaked up those coveted kisses. Smiled under their sweet rain and stared, stared into her eyes, past all that black makeup and sparkly powder.

Punk grrrls on all sides screamed their approval. Even the band was impressed. Hatchet growled on her mike, and Diesel winked at ME. Well, Cherry and me. Snatch did an amazingly long and loud drumroll and, after crashing the hell out of her cymbals, tossed her sticks into the crowd. Everyone was whistling and hooting and yelling for more. We were the superheroes in our own joyous, punkrawk comic strip.

Cherry hopped off me and wiped her forehead with her sleeve. She grabbed me and we headed to the bar for big glasses of water.

"Where's Carlotta?" I yelled. Even though the band wasn't playing, my ears rang and buzzed.

"You mean Carl? FaggityFag Carl?"

"I mean Carlotta. Don't be a jerk, Cherry."

"Probably blowing Pretty Boi in the bathroom. They never mosh!"

I kept my eyes peeled, but I couldn't see them in the crowd. I squinted and stared, trying to catch a glimpse of Carlotta or of Carol and her long, blonde hair. I hoped for gold flicking over her shoulder or swinging at her waist. Nowhere. But I did see Hardcore Hank and his seven inches of orange Mohawk. He was across the room, arguing with the bar manager about something or other, and just when it looked like it might get serious, he slapped the guy on the back, friendly-like, and bought him a shooter. That's Hardcore Hank for you.

When I turned back to Cherry, she was flirting with a big, drunk jock. She asked him for a cigarette. He slurred, "Only if you sit and smoke with me," and dug around in the pocket of his university jacket. It said *Engineering* across the back in raised letters. The guy was obviously wasted because his pack was right there on the bar, with a dorky lighter that said *True Blue: I Support the Metro Police*. Cherry helped herself and lit one.

"I've got smokes, you know," I said.

She snorted and patted her hair, did her best Mae West. "Save 'em for later, Dollface. Femme fatale at work."

Cherry hopped on the guy's barstool and swung her legs toward him. He was delighted that someone from the planet Girl was visiting. He didn't like the music and he found the clientele scary. Especially the females. He said he lost his frat brothers on their pub crawl and somehow ended up here, in Satan's Playhouse, alone and hammered. I glared at him but Cherry seemed fascinated. She leaned closer, planted a knockout smile in his face as she introduced herself.

"You girls are freaky. You're hot, but, like, your friend? Why does she do that to her hair?" he asked, contempt on his face.

I said, "So guys like you don't confuse me for someone who gives a shit. Why are you even here, if you don't like it?" Maybe I was being a bit aggressive, but I mean really! This was our place. Or at least it would be when we had our fake ID. I knew Hardcore Hank wouldn't let anything bad happen. He'd pulverize this guy if he touched even one erect hair on my otherwise bald head.

Cherry clapped her hands and said, "Rob, so, now we should have a drink together. I want a vodka tonic and so does my friend Simone, and you should buy them because, see, you hurt her feelings."

I said, "Don't bother. Come on, Cherry. Let's go." But no, she wasn't ready to go.

Mister University said, "I'll buy you a drink 'coz you're sexy. Not her," pointing at me. "You should come back to the frat, Red, and we'll show you how to really party." Rob leered at her and belched. Cherry giggled.

I turned away and focused on the stage, trying to ignore DorkAss, who just lit the wrong end of his cigarette. What killed me is how obviously he thought he was getting laid. Why Cherry wasted even ten minutes on this guy was beyond me. He turned to order from the bar and I said, "Why'd you tell him my name?" And, "I'm not missing the next set just so you can get free drinks from some stoopid guy."

She said, "You know I have a thing for frat boys."

"Since when?" I said.

"Since they're easy and stupid and rich. Duh!"

Smiling, she took the drink, compliments of You-Know-Who. She gave me the distant, "I'm on the job" look and rubbed her knee on his jeans. Upper thigh, near his zipper. Job or no, it seemed wrong to me, after all our moshing.

All those kisses.

"Screw that," I said, and pushed my way through the crowd, heading back to the stage.

chapter six

Exit Light

Let's face it, the pit rocked but it was a bit of a letdown after ruling with Cherry. The girls were still down in there, mixing it up, but not in the overpowering, separatist kind of way like before. I sweated and crashed around with everyone, let the music take me away. I ate up those sexy chicks on stage. I kept hoping You-Know-Who would get tired of her latest dinkfest and jump back in. I got an elbow in the back of the head so I whipped around to punch whoever, but it was Hardcore Hank. I gave him a smooch on the lips instead.

"Hey, Freaky," he yelled. "Hardcore Hank at your cervix!" He was double fisting the Fifties and he chugged one of the bottles now, so he could be rid of it. He threw it and we heard a smash of glinting glass as it hit the edge of the stage. A cheer went up from the crowd.

"Yay, Hank." I was so happy to see him. He was big and tough and he knew everybody in the place, more or less. Hank wrapped a thoroughly tattooed arm around me and rubbed the shaved sides of my head like I was some little kid or something. Then he tried to head-butt me with his huge spikes.

"Easy, Hank," I said. "It's only fun 'til someone loses an eye."

He swayed and a perfumed cloud of booze rolled off of him. He was hammered. He was wearing his sleeveless *CBGBs* shirt over a washboard belly that you could sometimes get a peek at since the arm holes were ripped right down to where the shirt tucked into tight pants that molded down to his studded, pointy-toed boots. Studded leather gauntlets covered his forearms and he was wearing at least ten pounds of hardware in chains and knives on his silver biker belt.

We bounced around together until Hank spilled too much beer, so that was the end of that. "Fucking Hell," he said and chugged from his bottle. "I'm gonna find some cute girl to sit on." At the end of that song, when he whistled long and loud with his fingers in his mouth, shredding my eardrums, I noticed he was missing part of his canine tooth. Then off he went, staggering through the pit toward the back of the club where the merchandise table was and a few broken chairs.

Hardcore Hank had been around forever. He played guitar in a bunch of punk bands and I guess over the years he'd pretty much seen it all. Guys like Hank got beer bellies eventually, and a bit rough around the chops. They also got more scars and newer, better tattoos. People said he had the same hairstyle fifteen years ago, and probably the same style of boots, too. The girls kept getting younger, but Hank and his buddies weren't budging.

After a few more songs, I emerged for a breather. It was about twelve-thirty and I was heading for the can when I ran smack into Cherry. She was freaking. She grabbed my arm and made a beeline for the back fire exit.

"Come on, Simone."

"What?"

"Cops! Run!"

She pulled me through the crowd. That's when I heard the scuffle breaking out back over by the main entrance. I could see Rob over my shoulder. He was pointing at us and yelling. It looked like his friends found him, 'coz there were about three other huge Frat Fucks in matching jackets. They were charging our way but got trapped on the other side of a mass of people in total confusion. Everyone who was holding was trying to get the hell outta there. Hank appeared in a flash, and pulled us along to the back door, the service door that most people didn't know about. In the sea of faces, suddenly there was Carlotta's, perfectly made up and framed by her long, black hair. I grabbed a handful of silky ink. Carlotta turned to swing at me, but luckily Hank was still sweeping us along through the crowd and I wasn't in target range. Carlotta really packs a punch. She saw me, covered her mouth all "whoopsie" like, and fishtailed after us. Pretty Boi was right behind her, eyes wide and rimmed in dark liner with spiky, midnight blue hair.

Hank kept his eyes on the cops at the main door and told the four of us to run, that he'd cover for us. He kicked open the security door and we were gone, across the parking lot that was deserted except for some guys smoking a joint in one corner. When they saw us book it out of the club, they took off up the fire escape and into the next building through an open window. We ran straight for the ten-foot, chain-link gate at the back. I was thinking to kick it open until I noticed the shiny new padlock.

"*Puta*, it's locked!" yelled Carlotta.

I slowed for a second. Cherry sped ahead in a black leather blur. The glittering, iron-on, cherry patch streaked and clouded my peripheral vision. I faltered, staring at the shining clasp just hanging there, mocking us. Then I heard the back exit door fly open and I could hear Hank yelling something and other things being yelled back at him, and over top of it all, one deep voice.

"Freeze. Police."

Woodsy snare.

Leghold trap.

Jail bait.

chapter seven

Escape from Satan's Playhouse

Boot up, grab with both hands, and climb, climb, climb.

I barked orders like a sadistic commanding officer to block out the shouts of the cops and Cherry's bratty taunts. Pretty Boi lifted Carlotta up as high as his long tattooed arms let him and she scaled the top, in spite of her platform boots. Then he was up and over in two shakes, like he was in some military training camp or something. He helped Carlotta down the rest of the way on the other side. Two cops raced across the lot and fuck it if I didn't have my goddamned fishnets stuck on the top barby part. The worst was the swinging over, way up there, thigh ripped to a bloody mess. The fence shimmied and slapped against the support posts and there I was, an under-aged kebab, raw meat dripping.

Below, Cherry folded down her corset and flashed the cops. She threw my mother's shoulder pads over the fence, then pranced off, wolf howling as she ran into the dark alley behind Carlotta and Pretty Boi. As her laughter faded, I heard her yell, "Mothahfuckah!" one more time. I saw the last dregs of Hank as another cop hauled him back into the bar and closed the door behind them. Finally, like a year later, I jumped down and landed hard on my ankle.

My right leg buckled. Pain shot through that mass of ankle bone and I was alone and I couldn't move. The cop closest to me yelled from the other side of the fence. He said, "Stupid Hole," and "Bitch." He stopped in front of the fence and pulled his gun out of the holster. His breath came heavily. His eyes were close set. His smile was violent.

I was transfixed.

The other one called out, "Forget it, Steve. Not worth the paperwork." His voice wavered in forced camaraderie and I suddenly knew that he was also afraid of Steve.

Officer Steve was a dangerous man. Steve spat through the fence and it landed on my cheek, a goobery, hot hork that trickled down, searing a pathway to my studded collar.

Its frothy wetness broke the spell. I turned and half-lunged, half-limped away.

He yelled, "You're going to pay, got that?"

His voice was even and lethal and it followed me down the alley, chilling me to the bone.

chapter eight

Chillin'

I hobbled down the alley on my injured leg. I kept expecting RoboCop to pop up from behind, to grab at my swollen ankle like in some horror movie—but no. I stayed in the shadows and crept into the empty lot that led to the park. I worried they'd pull up in a cop car, party lights blurring and siren wailing. But reason told me there'd be enough business for them back at the club. Between the endless liquor license infractions and major coke dealing in the back room, they'd have their hands full.

I hoped Velvetine got out safely.

I heard Carlotta's signature laugh and a high pitched shriek from Cherry. I didn't see them right away, until they waved me over. I'd been sweating in the pit and during the escape mission. I smelled a bit whiffy, even to myself. I collapsed near them on the grass, trying to catch my breath. My cheeks felt hot but the rest of my skin was shivery cold, hands clammy. Cherry was still laughing. She hiccupped. She rolled around under a large tree and kicked her legs up in the air a few times.

"Score!" Cherry did her personal victory dance, shaking invisible pom-poms in time with her butt. She pulled Frat Boy Rob's smokes and his crappy cop lighter out from the top of her left boot. The bulge in her right boot turned out to be his wallet. She tapped out a smoke, and when she did, a tiny plastic bag fell out, too. It was a forty bag. A half gram of coke.

"Wow," said Cherry. "Super score!" She tossed the cigarette to me and I lit it while she danced around with the bonus prize. "Who's in?"

Carlotta said, "Why not?" But me and Pretty Boi didn't say a thing because we hate coke. Carlotta said, "Only Cherry would *tief* some guy in the middle of a *puerco* cop raid," and we all laughed a bit, but then I got a memory flash of Rob and his drunken university friends, the way they were looking at us, so pissed. And then that other monster's face and the feel of his hot spit on my skin freaked me into silence.

Cherry took off her leather vest and smoothed it on the grass. She settled down and pulled out a small mirror from the pocket and a razor blade tucked into a tiny mother of pearl case. She tapped out the powder, cutting it up and forming wee lines on the mirror. She was singing an old song by the Pixies, off-key but still pretty. I lay back under the big tree, under the great sky canopy, and smoked. Tiny moonbeams filtered through the leaves and speckled her skin. There was one strip on a high cheekbone and one slithering down her long neck and one smudged right on her juicy, full bottom lip.

Pretty Boi pulled Carlotta onto his lap and kissed the top of her head. He hugged her to his chest. Carlotta stretched out her long legs and crossed them at the ankles. Her boots weighed in at about four pounds each, huge leather monstrosities with silver detailing and giant heels. They molded to her gorgeous calves, nestled below the knee, and perfectly accessorized her striped, thigh-high stockings. She fixed her miniskirt and smiled a luscious, red-lipped smile up to him. She was tracing the shadow of his cheekbone down to his lips with a manicured nail.

Pretty Boi noticed me rubbing my sore ankle, trying to work out the kinks.

"Simone, you okay?"

Pretty Boi talks kind of out the side of his mouth. He has a beautiful, low, rumbly voice that matches his super-model body and he speaks with a deliberate quality that really gets your attention. Words fall past those gorgeous lips warm and neat, and if they had a color they'd be amber. Amber like his eyes and like a bottle of Jack Daniels that you sip and hold in your mouth.

"Yeah," I said. "Guess so."

He was wearing his faded red *Conflict* shirt with a giant *Meat is Murder* pin in front and patched up, cutoff army pants with combat boots. Tons of studded and beaded bracelets laced both forearms. His hoodie was tied around his waist so when he stood up and twirled around, it kind of looked like he was wearing a skirt.

"Hey," I said. "Did I ever tell you you're the prettiest boy I know?"

He smiled big and galloped over, pouted a bit and said, "Simone hurt her footie."

"No rumba for you," said Carlotta.

Cherry rolled up a five-dollar bill, tiny and tight, and used it to snort a line. Then she passed it to me. I shook my head *No*. Carlotta did a line. Pretty Boi hates coke more than me, but he didn't say anything about it since Carlotta hates him smoking and he can't seem to quit.

Even Steven.

"Come on, Simone, it's like a shooter," said Cherry. "Besides, it's free." When I didn't jump on the offer, she said, "Suit yourself," and snorted up the third line, too. "That's good shit," she said.

Pretty Boi and I lay back and shared a cigarette. At last I could relax a bit and look up into the night sky and see a few stars instead of that creepy cop's face. The city was alive all around us but we were invisible in this grassy island. Just us four and the ants and the pregnant alley cats, swaggling bellies in the shadows.

Cherry and Carlotta danced around and pointed out constellations they knew. Big Dipper. Orion's Belt.

"Fuck, Simone, your leg is a mess." Pretty Boi inspected the ugly scrape and the oozing blood. "Geez."

I looked and, to be honest, it was terrible. But right then I couldn't feel it much. A tingling only. I knew it would be throbbing soon.

Then Cherry remembered the stolen wallet and leapt over to rummage through it. "Thirty-eight dollars and seventeen cents," she announced. "Plus a two-for-one pizza coupon, and some girl's phone number. *Cheryl.* Maybe I'll call her," she laughed.

Even though I hated the guy, this didn't feel right to me. Cherry sifted through a bunch of bank cards, a student card with Robert Morley's ugly mug on it. Library card, driver's license, VISA. There was a condom in there, still sealed, shiny and hopeful. She gave it to Carlotta.

"Gracias, hermana."

Cherry held up a tiny key with an orange handle, labeled number forty-seven.

"Oh, look—the key to his heart," she said. She dingled it around and giggled. "Wonder what's in there?"

My fingers itched just looking at it. It made me curious, that key. Cherry kept twirling it around. She tossed it up and down, balanced it on her forehead, let it slip around and drop back into her hands. Her eyes glinted at me knowingly but she kept the orange thing tight in her fist. It was one of those locker keys from a bus station or a storage place. Something like the place my mom and I had to keep our stuff for a while. After we ran away from the voices in her head, while we stayed at the women's shelter. During our dramatic escape to Nowhere. For the longest time after that I used to keep a small emergency bag in a private locker of my own. Just in case.

What would a guy like him keep in a place like that?

Storage spaces got used by middle-aged men, thrown out by their wives, who had no place to keep all their crap. Bowling trophies, golf bags, suits zipped up in plastic. Folks without houses still had armfuls of treasure that they'd store away and come to visit every now and then. I tried to imagine the secrets they hoarded, tucked away in their own metal boxes. The tragic stories that lead them there. It fascinated me, I guess.

Cherry knew this, of course, and that's why she flaunted the thing, kept it away from me, but continued to play with it. I couldn't take my eyes off it.

"Thirty-eight bucks, huh?" said Carlotta.

Pretty Boi sat back down behind her, cuddling and braiding a little strand of her hair.

"Plus three drinks, a new lighter, and half a pack of smokes," said Cherry. "Not to mention the drugs. Wannanother line?"

She didn't wait for Carlotta's answer but poured out some more onto the little mirror and started the ritual over again.

"Pretty cool in the pit, eh?" I said and Cherry stopped for a minute to look at me and smile. Then she tapped with the razor a bit more. While Carlotta snorted a line, Cherry casually dropped the key in the grass by my foot. She pretended not to notice when I pocketed it, along with some of his ID. A few drops of moonlight dribbled down the bare skin of her arm. The top of her knobby spine looked weirdly holy. She smiled again at me, and that was an extra gift, the beautiful, shiny bow that went on top.

Later, Cherry sniffed loudly and rubbed at her nose. She swallowed loudly. She got bored and restless. She ripped out grass in handfuls, threw it around on me. The night air around her was charged with negative particles and I didn't know why.

So I said, "Quit it, Cherry."

She dumped another load on my head.

Cherry said, "So *now* what are we doing?"

Pretty Boi said, "*Mi amor?*"

And Carlotta said, "Me and Pretty Boi are taking off so I can jump his bones, eh, *Vato?*"

Pretty Boi smiled wide and his eyes shone and next thing you know, Carlotta straddled him right there and they started making out all over the place.

Then Cherry got in a snit and said she was outta there, it sucked, and it was her first night free from the confines of junior jail high school, or something like that, and was I gonna lame out on her or was I up for a real party? And I didn't answer at first because I was busy watching Carlotta and Pretty Boi kiss and move around a bit and they looked just like the movies.

chapter nine

Now What?

Around 3 a.m. Cherry was walking and I was limping along the back streets, heading down to the east harbor. Cherry wanted to hit the Bikers' Boozecan, and I didn't. I wanted to go to a house party, one the Cuntagion crew would be at. She was arguing back, "It's my fucking Prom night, so no." She was sniffing and humming. She stuck her pinky in the tiny empty bag, and rubbed her gums. She wanted more.

"We should pass by Hank's place. He's probably pretty worried."

"I can't wait to start making some money," she said, ignoring me completely.

"I have a bad feeling about this, Cher," I said. "Let's go home. I'll totally party with you this weekend. My treat, okay?" I kept looking over my shoulder, thinking with my luck we'll run into that Demented RoboCop again.

"No, Simone, it's not okay. I lined up this job thingy and you didn't do anything to help, if I remember correctly. The least you can do is go with me. We're not gonna see the frat guy or his friends, and definitely not some creepy pig. I'm not in school anymore and fuck if I'm getting some grease pit job at McNasties. This is gonna be my job, for real, and you can just quit your whining right now."

"I'm not whining," I said, sulky.

"And quit limping. If you'd done a couple of lines you wouldn't even feel that right now," she said, righteously.

First of all, Cherry wanted a job like she wanted a kick in the pants. She wanted more coke and knew she'd be able to score some freebies, at least a quarter gram, at the Boozecan. Second, she never lined up anything except a good time. After we left Pretty Boi and Carlotta grinding in the park, she accidentally found a business card in her vest pocket that some creep had given her, who knew when. He'd tried to convince her to pose for some striptease Web site or something, and she'd only listened long enough to figure out that he wasn't buying. She'd promptly stuffed the card in her pocket and that was it. Now she was making out as though the whole point of dropping by the Boozecan was to hook up with Web Porno Guy. Like it was an official Job Interview or something.

The little houses we passed were quiet, the windows dark. Here and there we heard voices spiraling out from shadowy front porches, or lofting down from hidden balconies, high above our heads. Our steps echoed against the rows of hous- es. Cherry's boots slapped an even beat but mine strayed from her dominant rhythm, tippling heavy on the one side, dragging the right slightly, and both were slower than hers. Occasionally we landed in synch but more often our footfalls strayed apart and that seemed to irritate Cherry, which caused me some anxiety.

I couldn't keep up.

Finally, I saw a gnarled branch that had fallen beside the sidewalk. I picked it up and used it as a walking stick and it eased the weight from my sore ankle quite a bit.

"You better ditch that thing before we get near the door," she said. "Geez, you look like an old man."

Just then we heard the rattling muffler of a car coming up behind us, and a lone wolf whistle sailing over the sounds of some loud music.

I said, "Shit."

Cherry actually flipped her pigtails and cocked her head to see who it was. I readied myself with the stick, now an ancient weapon yearning to crack skulls and trip up enemies in battle.

A deep voice called out, "All right, Baby Girl. Wass up, Freaky?"

This guy was practically hanging out of his friend's car by the gonads, trying to work some magic through his bulging biceps with a gangsta rap soundtrack. Cherry sashayed over to the car which was now filling the previously quiet street with a toxic blue exhaust, not to mention some serious noise pollution. I saw a light flick on across the street.

She said, "Room in there for two?"

I poked her with my stick. "Cherry!" But her mind was already made up.

"See, my friend hurt her foot and we need a ride to our party," she said and shot me a warning look. Mister Man and Cherry kept looking each other up and down until I thought for sure their eyeballs would fall right out, roll down their fronts, across the road and right into the fucking gutter. Two extra pairs of eyes blinked from inside the car. Optical semaphore.

What's in it for us? They were wondering.

Nothing. That's what my squinty eyes said back.

They staked and surveyed a three-pointed area on my torso, the fertile farmlands of my own Bermuda Triangle. Then they turned away, uninterested in my meager wares or my irrelevant protests.

"Get in." Cherry grabbed the stick and whipped it across the street. Then she stuffed me in the back seat behind Thing One and beside Thing Two, both of whom were apparently competing in the Who Can Wear the Most Cologne Contest.

"Guess I'll have to sit right up here with you." Cherry hovered above Guy Smiley's muscular crotch and then settled carefully.

I passed him a tissue and made a helpful gesture towards my own chin.

"Eh?" he said.

"Bit . . . of . . . drool." I was speaking slowly and smiling like I meant it.

The driver cranked the tunes even louder and sparked up a huge celebratory cone while I tried to shout directions to the not-so-secret location of the club. He exhaled the fragrant smoke and passed the blunt to Thing Two, who hesitated before offering me some of it.

"What's with the Do?" he said, meaning my hairdo, I guessed. Then he started yelling, "Anarchy in the UK! Hey, Punk Is Dead! Ha ha har."

I said, "Something like that."

By the time we pulled into the correct alley I had a severe kink in my neck from trying to not let my head bump into the huge speaker in the corner, and also from being squashed down on the seat so my hair could fit in without bending or breaking on the low upholstered ceiling. On top of that, I was trying to keep a rabid eye on the activity in the front seat. Rambo had made himself somewhat acquainted with the beauty mark on Cherry's inner thigh, but hadn't been able to figure out how to unclick the garters. It confirmed my High Sperm Count, Low IQ suspicion.

"You a dyke?"

I took it as a friendly inquiry and nodded.

"Thanks for the ride," I said. "And the smoke."

Then we waited an eternity while Mr. Man wrote out his number on a piece of cardboard from somebody's cigarette pack. "Maybe we'll stop by later," he grunted. "Check things out."

Cherry untangled herself and waved as they gunned it down the street.

"He's a hottie, eh?"

I said, "Not exactly my type."

I was picturing the whole car driving clear off the marina dock, exploding over a cliff, falling down a giant manhole, cartoon-style, a hundred times over.

"I got us a ride here, didn't I?"

Cherry was all sparkly and weird from the rush and I thought, *Oh no, not again.* "Think they'll come back?" she asked excitedly. She was twirling the piece of paper with his number on it between her fingers like she did his tiny braids a few minutes earlier.

"Think they'd get in? They're not exactly bikers," I said, all sullen.

"Cockblocker," she said. "Tonight is Cherry's Prom. Cherry's night out, not Lesbo night out. Okay?"

Okay.

chapter ten

After Hours

Godzilla whisked us inside and bolted the unmarked metal door behind us.

"Purse."

Big, hairy, man hands motioned for me to spread, then frisked their way around looking for weapons, bottles of booze, whatever. He stirred a long finger into Cherry's purse and gave us a cranky nod. We walked down a long, unpainted hallway to the second Monster's drawbridge. Luckily I recognized that Troll, so the check was pretty brief. He knew we were underaged and all, but like he cared. The whole thing was illegal so it wasn't like our little teenaged butts were their only problem. Besides, the younger and prettier the girls were, the more the guys spent on booze and drugs.

After the frisking and patting down, all friendly-like, we jostled our way into the crowded main room and stood around in line waiting to pay way too much money for a warm can of Budweiser. The music was loud rock and metal hits from the past century and nobody was dancing. People stood around in bunches or sat in mismatched furniture, talking, laughing, arguing. Whatever. The back room was in steady use and the security guy on that door was tripping out, neurotically picking fights with anyone who looked at him the wrong way. I sipped beer and Cherry made frantic trips around the place, searching for anyone she knew, or anyone who had some free drugs for her. Typical.

Some biker dude really wanted to convince me that I was straight.

"Why'd you do that to your hair? You'd be kind of pretty. Like with long hair. Something." He leaned back on his boot heels and opened a new can of beer. It foamed over and dripped down over his fingers. Then he licked it up. "Check that!" he said. "Check that tongue action, sweetheart!"

I said, "Thanks, dude. You'd be kind of pretty, too. Like if you grew two boobs and had a full body wax." I smiled a dazzler and left him standing there, licking his own fingers.

I found Cherry practically sitting in some slimeball's lap. The guy was checking her out but blowing her off at the same time. I'd seen him around before, in the clubs and outside, dealing in Punker Park. I was surprised that Cherry seemed to know him. His name was Vincent and he was way older than us. Like way in his twenties at least. Maybe even thirty! He had shiny, pointy-toed boots, tight pants, and some shiny club shirt. His bleach-blond dreads hung to his shoulders and he was very thin. At a distance he looked like some dude in a cool rock band maybe, but up close, he seemed sleazy. A bit sinister. That's what I thought, anyway. He had a young rottweiler pup with him on a sort of thick chain. She kept tugging to investigate doggy smells and meet other people and that sort of thing, but Vincent didn't like that. He'd jerk her back close and shove her flat to the concrete floor with his boot holding her down. I hated that. And it made me hate him, right away, down to the core. But not Cherry. She didn't notice those things about him. She noticed that he had money and lots of drugs and that the women at the party all wanted to get with him, and that made her want him more. All the men deferred to him. Everyone knew who he was. That was more than enough for her—and that's how Cherry fell in love.

Bam.

She perched up high on the arm of the chair next to him, leaned forward, tried to keep his attention with some animated story or other. She got him to light her cigarettes, like the other girls. True, she sometimes had to ask him more than once, but it didn't dissuade her. Not one bit. I wondered if he could tell the difference between the girls who just wanted stuff off him and Cherry, who loved him and also wanted stuff off him. Cherry had definitely scored since we got there. I could tell from watching her, she was so wired. And although I whispered that I wanted to leave, that I had to get some sleep and that I didn't like the vibe in the place, she refused. I was desperate to get her away from him, to stop this train wreck I knew was going to happen.

"I'm sure, I just met the hottest guy here and I'm partying with him for, like, two seconds and you want to ruin it. Whateve."

"Dude's ugly," I said.

Then she said, "Jealous much, Simone?" and I wondered, was I?

Of course I was! I'd only loved her since grade seven. I'd only been her faithful schlep, the eternal sidekick, the bodyguard, her loveless slave for ever. And there'd been nights when it had seemed possible, when she would settle down and tuck in with me and whisper secrets and dreams and tell jokes and stories and draw designs on my back and kiss my neck until I fell asleep. There were always hints and possibilities and I'd waited around for them like a kicked stray, nosing for scraps at the table.

"Can I pet your dog?" I asked Vincent, the Master of All Evil.

And he goes, "She doesn't like other bitches. Can't you tell?" and put his arm around Cherry. She stuck her tongue out at me and off they went into the back room,

Ugly Vincent, Heartless Cherry, and the little dog, too.

There I was, drunk and devastated, sitting in some ratty, oversized chair, thinking *Now fucking what?* I should've left right then, but I was afraid for Cherry. For what might happen to her if she were left behind with all those guys. That's what I was telling myself, although later Carlotta would say,

"*Puta*, you should've been scared for those *pobres hombrecitos*." And some irrational part of me kept thinking that as long as I was there witnessing it all, I could have some say in how things went down. That I'd have some amount of control, however minute.

In hindsight, there was a darker, more twisted part of me that just wouldn't let go of her. It sat, crouched and hopeful, enduring the next kick and the next, in case there might be another kiss somewhere down the road.

The party was still going strong but it seemed like the clientele had changed to an older, crustier crowd, and the young girls had left and the women still hanging around were different. Way older and tougher and skinny and twitchy. Cracked out. Nobody I knew, that's for sure. People huddled in small groups, freebasing to heaven and back, right out in the open, and everything jumped up a notch or two. The voices got louder, more shrill, and people gesticulated wildly as they talked and laughed and slapped each other on the shoulders. After a while, the air seemed charged with negative energy and once again, I was frozen in my spot. A fistfight broke out over some money owed, but it ended after the guy who wanted the money slammed the other guy's head down, hard, face first onto a table top. Blood gushed from his nose and then he was dragged out by Godzilla and Barred For Life.

That's when I felt it, a soft nudge on my knee and a whiskery tickling with warm air. I jumped a bit but it was just that little puppy, nuzzling me and saying hello. She had trotted out from the back room, chain dragging behind her, and no one had noticed. She looked up at me with velvet brown

61

eyes, like dark chocolate pools, and her dangling, hilarious tongue made her look like she was smiling. I blinked at her and she blinked back. She went over to the chair Ugly Vincent had been sitting in, squatted, and peed a good size puddle on the floor. Then she hopped up on the chair I was in, turned around a couple times, and promptly fell asleep with her head in my lap.

Desolate and abandoned, I cherished her the way any loser does the consolation prize.

chapter eleven:

Cherry's Place

"Wow, look," I said.

Cherry staggered to the railing and lurched over it.

"Whoah. What a giant rat."

"No, not down there, Cherry. Look up. The sunrise."

A faint, pink glow had invaded the silver sky. From the fire escape outside her bedroom window, we could see the whole neighborhood right up to the bridge with the train tracks. Bright licks of light filtered in between the buildings and over rooftops, warming us even as we stood there. A few stray stars still hung in the early morning sky.

"It's pretty, eh?" I smiled, and let this picture gloss over top of all those others, those uglier ones from our long night. "Remember when we used to make forts out here and have sleepovers?"

She said, "God, this is killing my eyes. I must be part vampire. Sunrise is evil tide." She collapsed on the window ledge and started to undo the laces of her huge boots. "Roll a joint."

"Cherry." I swear she never knew when to quit.

"Roll it."

I noticed her face was gray and her eyes looked flat. She wiped her clammy palms on her mini-kilt and I saw that her hands were shaking.

Chemical OverLoad.

I said, "What were you doing with that guy? You don't look so hot."

"Fucking roll it or I'll puke again. I'm out of coke."

"Coke? Or crack. 'Coz it looked like you were smoking crack with your new ghetto friends."

I didn't even mention how I'd walked in on them by accident, Vincent standing in the washroom, hands all over Cherry, with her back to me. He'd stared right at me, the prick, daring me to . . . *what?* What could I do? She wanted to be there with him, I knew that much, so I'd left quietly. I waited outside under the dying night sky with Lucette, his sleepy puppy, and when Cherry came out I traded her back for the dog. Vincent took up the dog chain and gave Cherry a little kiss and a push in my direction. He hopped in his crappy Honda Civic and drove off. He had left us in the parking lot by the harbor at five-thirty a.m., left me to limp and drag her a million miles by foot, 'til we got to a 24-hour bus route.

"Fuck you, Simone. You're no fun." Cherry leaned forward with a dry heave.

Me No Fun? Nothing was fun anymore.

It was like trying to feed a hunger in her that wouldn't quit. It reeked of desperation, and it scared me. I scraped up my last bit of herb and tapped it onto the fragile papers. I rolled it up slowly and carefully.

Cherry's Prom. Really Fun.

"Cherry," I said. "Remember the time we went camping and rented a canoe and paddled around in that lake? Now that was fun. We should do that again. Remember the lake?" I thought if I could get her away from this place, away from that guy and the parties and the drugs, just for a few days even, that things could be different.

"For fuck's sake, shut up and roll the fucking joint!"

Cherry's face was whitewhite and her eyes were dangerous. She sucked back the last swig of bourbon from the silver flask she kept tucked in her garter and almost brought it right back up.

I finished sealing the joint and skipped making a tiny cardboard filter. I tossed it over to her and, without a word, pushed past her through the open window and sat on her messy bed. I could hear her out there trying to light the damn thing but her matches kept going out. I knew, as well as I knew my own name, I was supposed to lean out and light it for her with my Zippo. These unspoken rules existed long before I ever noticed them, and I'd only realized that very night that I hated them.

Let FuckFace Vincent light your stoopid joint, I thought.

Instead I sat on top of the crumpled pink bedspread and held the lighter in my fist. I exhaled and dropped it onto the carpet. Then I started unlacing my boots, pulling and loosening. I tugged the right one off first and gasped with pain. I peeled down the sock carefully and looked at the swollen and bruised ankle.

Shit!

When I took off the other boot a lump fell out. The key! The frat guy's ID. I'd forgotten all about it. I stacked it up on the bedside table and set her cruddy alarm clock, to get up for school in two hours. I closed my eyes and was out, fast asleep at the foot of Cherry's bed, curled up fetal. Dreamless.

When I opened my eyes, the alarm had been going for some time.

"Shit!" I was late for math class and had a spare second period. I'd get there in time for history, and lunch.

A dead weight kept me flat on my back. Cherry's left boot was resting happily across my neck. I had a super big close-up of the smelly laces and stitching that wandered around the leather, and of the fishnet stocking that sagged around her knee. She moved slightly, dreaming maybe, and her booted leg jumped, clocking the side of my face. No wonder my head hurt. I shook her leg away, pushed it off, and sat up.

The sun was hot and merciless though the open window, but her other boot was propped up on the sill, miraculously creating a rectangle of shade for her pale face. She rubbed her head deeper into the pillows, arms stretched out on either side, wearing nothing but her red PVC collar and the Sacred

Heart panties, one fishnet stocking and a boot. A real live punk rock crucifix. A regular blowup doll splayed on the bed.

My head pounded and my tongue felt huge and furry in the dried-out cavern of my mouth. I was sweating and the bedroom walls taunted me with their garish pink paint and peeling rock posters that drooped like an old, saggy bra strap. The posters had changed, as had the piles of castoff clothes twisted ankle deep on the carpet and around the computer she stole from our school. Otherwise, Cherry's room looked exactly as it had since grade seven when she and her mom painted it together. The shelf above her bed still held a whole whack of stuffed animals, dolls with missing limbs, and a ceramic, pink piggy bank, recently emptied to scrape up bus fare.

I staggered out to the bathroom and noticed Cherry's mom passed out on the couch, wearing a ratty negligee.

The apple doesn't fall far from the tree.

Their tiny bathroom was like a convection oven, so I cranked open the window and scared off a couple of pigeons. I piled my smoky clothes on top of closed lid of the toilet and carefully stepped into the chipped enamel tub. I let the cool water do its magic. I stood there forever, soaking my hair and washing away all that dirt. The water brought me back to life, well soaped and shining.

When the pipes finally clanged out their warning, I turned off the tap and pushed back the goldfish-patterned shower curtains. I'd bought them at the Dollar Store. Mainly because I couldn't stand the old moldy ones that were up there. Those were the kinds of things that Cherry and her mom never got around to doing. The boring old day-to-day things like getting toilet paper and new toothbrushes once in a while.

I sipped water, and gathered up my belongings. I waltzed down the hallway in a green towel. It had a large bleach stain on it. It was a tie-dye disaster. I was humming a song by the Smiths.

Girlfriend In a Coma.

I pushed open Cherry's bedroom door and froze. The man didn't know I was there. He was busy.

Cherry opened her eye and fixed it on me. She was looking at me but not seeing me. It was a blank stare from underneath his cowboy hat and sweat-stained cotton shirt. The little bed jiggled and squeaked.

My clothes fell to the floor, to join all those piles of things Cherry never picked up and put away. I grabbed the closest thing from the dresser. The Virgin of Guadalupe votive candle that Carlotta gave her.

I held it high and stepped towards the bed. I brought the Virgin down on the back of his head. Not once. Not twice. I don't know.

"Stupid!"

Cherry rolled him over the pink polyester cliff and glared at me. She pulled at the ripped panties which were tangled up along her boot and threw them down. Strangely enough, they fluttered and landed on his exposed crotch. Like a perverted game of horseshoes.

She said, "Now look what you've done."

Cherry stumbled over to her dresser and pulled on an old *Marilyn Manson* T-shirt.

"What the fuck am I supposed to do about this?"

She found her little red kilt under the window sill and tugged. It was partly stuck underneath the man. Cherry kicked at his shoulder until the skirt came free and waved it like a flag in my face.

"Well? Is he fucking dead or what?!"

Still I didn't say a word and she huffed her way around me and checked to see if he was breathing, put her fingers alongside his neck to feel a pulse.

"Come on," she said. "We're leaving."

She grabbed the candle from me and wiped the blood on the dingy curtain before tossing it onto his bloated stomach.

"Get dressed."

I moved like a robot. I dropped the towel, put on some of her clothes and some of mine. I made an outfit of it all, somehow. I scooped up Frat Guy's ID and the little orange key, and shoved them into my jacket pocket. I carried my boots into the cramped living room and sat on the edge of the couch to put them on. Cherry's mom groaned and turned in her sleep, nudging me off the furniture. So I sat on the floor and started lacing.

"God. What do I have to do to get some sleep around here?" Cherry stomped around, opening cupboards and the fridge, trying to find something to drink other than stale beer and vodka.

Cherry's mom opened her eyes and smiled at me vaguely.

"Hi honey. Are you going to school?"

I stared back at her.

"Oh, you girls and your boots. Good thing there isn't a fire." She rubbed her face and sat up. She looked around the room in confusion and then adjusted her negligee. "Anyone seen Frank?"

Cherry plowed into the room and lit a cigarette. "Oh, as a matter of fact, yes. We've seen a whole lot of Frank. Maybe you could try to keep your boyfriends in your own room from now on, Mom."

"What did you do to him?" She snapped alert.

"Don't look at me. Ask Aileen Wuornos here." Cherry blew smoke at my head.

"Honey, where's Frank?"

Cherry's mom leaned forward and I could smell her horrible breath. Somehow I found my voice and remembered how to make it work.

"You should be asking what Frank did to Cherry, not the other way around."

"Enough." Cherry kicked me to be quiet.

I stood up. I said, "Frank's lucky he's not dead. But if he ever touches Cherry again, he will be."

Cherry's mom's mouth dropped open. I stormed out, out of the apartment, down the seven flights of stairs, since the elevator was broken as usual, and out the front door.

A few minutes later the front door rattled behind me.

"Drama queen."

Cherry sat beside me on the stoop and smoked. She pulled out a cell phone and dialed a number. "Hey, Vincent, you Fox. It's Cherry. Cherry from last night. Call me back, okay? I got cash."

She never missed a beat.

"Where'd you get that phone?" I said

"Frank! Same place I got this," she laughed, and cracked his wallet out of her purse. It was thick with high end bills. She counted them out greedily, stacked them up, and there was about six hundred dollars. His disability cheque? She filed it away in her purse. Then she whipped out a compact powder case and drew thick black rings around her eyes and painted on eyebrows in two different colors.

I grabbed the mirror away and stared at her.

"What is wrong with you?" she said. "You're really getting on my nerves lately."

"Are you serious? I'm not the one smoking crack! I'm not the one who just got raped by your mother's pig boyfriend! And I'm the only one around here who seems to give a fuck. Did you even care what he was doing to you? Did you like it or something? I don't get it!"

She said, "Just drop it, okay?"

"Why should I fucking drop it? It makes me sick, you know that?"

Cherry looked me right in the eye and chose her words carefully. "Maybe Frank and I have an arrangement. Ever think of that? I have something Frank wants and Frank's wallet has something I want. And maybe deep down my mom somehow knows all about it and doesn't give a shit. So let's just leave it at that. Try not to bruise yourself up too much being a superhero or anything. Okay?"

Okay.

Then I went to school and Cherry didn't.

Cherry's Blog: Most Recent Entry
Thursday, May 22 1:45 PM

To everyone who bailed on Cherry's Prom . . . you suck.

To everyone who tried to have fun but couldn't because they were too busy being jealous and self-absorbed (ie Simone) . . . Grow UP.

To everyone who rocked and had fun last night, you know who you are . . . Me!

The band was great. So was the bar, until it got raided. But Cherry and the girls made a daring escape and a good time was had by all. Plus, I scored in more ways than one ☺☺ and definitely took it to the limit. I can't believe I don't feel worse today. Couple a rails fixed that up. Hair of the dog!

So, one decision, one night and suddenly my life is a completely new story. That's destiny, right? I never thought I'd be the type to fall for anyone, but there you go. V. is the hottest guy ever and he said he noticed me a long time ago, too, but he gets shy when he really likes someone (!) so he never talked to me. I thought it was because of my age (shhh) but he is not prejudiced like some people, and he says I'm really mature compared to other girls he knows. He is so cool. He makes me feel beautiful. I had the feeling that we already knew everything about each other before we even met. Like from a past life or something, if you believe in that. Sounds cheesy, I know, but that's how it is. I finally met my match: a real man who can push as hard as I can take it.

Now I'm going back to sleep since my alcoholic mother and the corpse finally left.

When I wake up it will be to my new, exciting life. No school, no bullshit.

Total me and total V.

Mood: Romantic and Tired. And Sore ☺
Music: Marcy Playground "Sex and Candy"

book two:

spiraLing

Cherry's Blog: Most Recent Entry

Thursday, May 29 6:37 am

I love sex with V. He just has to look at me in a certain way and I can hardly keep my hands off him. I love shocking him, love to torture him in public. Last night we were making out at the club and he was fiddling under the waist band of my skirt and his rings got caught on the elastic of my g-string. He was so curious that I described them in every last tiny detail. A while later, when he was trapped in the back corner pulling some deals or whatever, I sent the waitress over with a beer, his favorite kind, only I tied the g-string in a little bow around the neck of the bottle. I was leaning against the bar, directly across the room from him, watching the whole thing and it was such a rush to watch his face as he realized what the hell he was holding. He could hardly pay attention to the dudes there, just kept staring at me and I almost thought we didn't need to touch each other. Our eyes were doing a good enough job on their own. Not for long, though! We kept "accidentally" bumping into each other in line for the can, or out on the back fire escape. Each time we hardly said a word, just went at it, started up where we'd left off the time before, as soon as we had any privacy. I know he has LOTS of experience and everything, with all kinds of girls but he says I'm his best daredevil. He drove me home this morning and we did some more lines in the car right before you know what-ing, right in front of my building!

PS Guess who still has my panties?

Mood: Exhausted but Very High. Horny but a bit Sore.
Music: Marilyn Manson "Deformography"

chapter twelve:

Fountain of Youth

"Yo! Carlotta!"

She clomped toward me in triple-decker, high-heeled sneakers.

I was crashed out on the grass, overheated, and struggling out of my twenty-hole boots when she arrived. She dropped her huge purse and let out a sigh. Carlotta and I liked to meet at the fountain for lunch. It was hidden in this little concrete square, among a bunch of corporate office buildings. I tossed my boots aside and began methodically picking the sock fluffs from in between my toes. I removed my army pants and the heavy metal bullet belt that held them up. Then, ignoring the signs that warned otherwise, I hopped into the cool water and waded around in there, while Carlotta sat on the ledge.

Heaven.

A couple of Suits looked over with disgust, but kept talking on their important cell phones, tapping the soles of their designer shoes. If Cherry had been there, she would have shot them the finger.

"You know, the grass *is* way greener over here," I said. I twirled in the water wearing only a ripped up men's shirt, a tie, and a pair of boxer shorts. I surveyed the manicured lawn around us. It was bright green, evenly clipped, with marble benches and some interesting outdoor sculptures. At school, the lawn looked bad until you sat down. Then it looked terrible. You'd notice how it was really all bald patches of dusty dirt, and pieces of garbage. Lots of bugs. Plus, the only official place to sit was at the charred picnic table. It had half a bench and was covered in gang logos and bird shit. You couldn't move it to the shade because its wobbly legs were cemented into the ground.

"Hmm." Carlotta was renovating her face. She rifled through her bag for cosmetics and other surgical devices. "Shit, I got so much work to do," she said. "Why weren't you at school yesterday?"

"Pamela couldn't come by and my mom was having a rough day."

She'd been up two nights in a row searching for something, who knew what, tearing the cupboards and drawers apart. The apartment was a disaster. My terrified mother, hijacker and hostage both, kept us locked up all day, waiting for the voices to say something different. Something that might bode well for our future.

"Anyways," I said, " do you know what I mean about the grass?"

She wiped her forehead with a disposable face cloth and patted her face with a pink, Hello Kitty, powder puff. She reapplied her red lipstick, then gathered up her long silky hair and tied it in a knot on top of her head. It looked strange and sophisticated up there. Like a pineapple.

"Simone," she said. "Are you asking do I fucking know that poor folks who don't matter get shit while rich folks who work in big office buildings get everything?! Is that whatchoo mean?"

"Oh. Um . . . yeah." I hated sounding like such a naïve dork.

"Then, yes, I know *exactemente* what you mean. So does my mother, who's working another double to pay for our shitty, overpriced apartment, and so does *mi tia,* who's at the Wal-Mart with fake papers, trying to pay for daycare so she can work for minimum wage."

I watched her mop the back of her neck with another dainty, perfumed wipey thing. "Hot out, eh?"

Carlotta glared at me. She unlaced her shoes and splished her bare feet in the water halfheartedly. She was in a pretty bad mood.

"At least school's almost over," I said, hopefully.

"Not yet. I got to finish an English essay and study for finals, plus look after *mi familia.*" I smiled guiltily. Sometimes I plain forgot how other people lived, with kids and suppers and all those precious domestic routines. At Carlotta's there were two families, hers and her aunt's, sharing the one apartment. Two grown sisters, Carlotta, two teenaged boys, two twin seven-year-olds, and a baby. Two big families, minus the dads. Of course I had exams to study for, too, but that reality hadn't sunk in yet. Or maybe I already knew I'd be repeating a few classes next year.

"In September me and Pretty Boi are transferring to an alternative school so we can upgrade in one term. Then we're gonna work and save money for college. If the marks are good enough," she added.

"They will be. You're super smart, Carlotta."

"Thanks, *Gringa*." After a minute she said, "What are you gonna do later?"

"Tonight? Cherry got us a job interview or something. For some internet thing."

"No," she laughed. "Like later next year."

I chewed on my lower lip for a bit and splashed around some more. "I dunno. I guess you, Pretty Boi, Velvetine and Sexy Carol will be graduated. I'll be all alone."

"Ah, Carol." Carlotta looked at me slyly.

"Mmm, Sexy Carol." I blushed just saying her name. "Hey, why didn't she come to the Cuntagion show?"

"Working," said Carlotta. Then she said, "Simone, sometimes I worry about you. You got lots going on up there in *la cabeza* and you got to find something that makes you click, you know? Don't get stuck here. Why don't you change schools, too? Start over someplace new. They got all kinds of *lesbianas* downtown at that school." Carlotta undid her hair and let it fall, long, around her shoulders again.

"Hmm." It had never occurred to me that there was some choice in the matter. That things could maybe be different. Carlotta opened a window and let some breeze into the back corner of my mind and, even if I closed it, I'd have to acknowledge what I hadn't known existed before.

"Think about it, Simone."

Which would be hard, considering all I wanted to think about was summer and what I'd be doing for the next couple of months. I wanted to have fun, not Cherry's kind, but my own. I wanted to run or fight or mosh, anything. My body craved contact, my waking and sleeping minds couldn't shut off the hormonally charged dreams that mocked my shyness, my lack of experience with girls.

Carlotta gave me a kick.

"Huh?" I blushed ridiculously.

"I said, whaddup with Cherry? I read her live journal. Is she for real? I haven't seen her since Cuntagion. *Puta*, I haven't even gone out since that night. Close call, huh? Velvetine took off in a hurry when those *puercos* showed, and forgot her pants at the bar. She had to Hail Mary a cab in her nun costume . . . ha ha."

We laughed about that for a minute and then I turned my mind back to Cherry, to how I was gonna answer the question at hand. Cherry's social life had escalated at an alarming rate the past couple of weeks.

"If partying was a national sport, than Cherry is in Olympic training." That's what I said, anyway.

I still went out with her most nights since she hated going anywhere by herself, but if Vincent was there she didn't care when I left. I'd have a beer, go hang with Lucette outside. I'd throw sticks for her and play tag and we'd run around panting, until Vincent wanted her back. Cherry went anywhere Vincent would take her. After the bars closed for the night, she'd go to the after parties. Once you'd been to one, you'd get invited to another, and so on. She was getting to know all kinds of people. Bartenders and bouncers, two-bit actors and guys in bands. When Vincent was around they treated her carefully. They didn't look directly at her, even. If Vincent didn't take her, well, she'd find out where he was going and tag along with those other guys. Once in a while he'd show up with another girl on his arm and ignore Cherry altogether. Those were ugly nights. She was doing a shitload of coke, an eightball a night, easy, and I'd seen her freebasing more than a bit. She said she only smoked rocks when it was free, or when she ran out of powder. I had no idea where she slept. Not at her place, that's for sure. Sometimes I'd crawl in through her window and lock the bedroom door, push the dresser against it to keep the Franks out. I'd read her web journal updates and wait for her to come home. Mostly she didn't.

"Who's V.?" said Carlotta.

"Vincent," I said. "She hooked up with some dealer. That guy with the blond dreads, you know. I guess he's her boyfriend. Sort of."

"So you like him, eh?" Carlotta smiled her sarcasm at me.

"Actually, I hate him. But he's got a really pretty dog."

Carlotta laughed again and pushed me a bit, playfully.

"Seriously, her name's Lucette." Then I said, "Cherry parties hard every night, right, and I don't know. She's kind of out of control. She's one crazy girl."

"Cherry's not a girl. She's a nuclear weapon!" said Carlotta, and laughed big.

I smiled but felt sick. Everything was going wrong and no one else seemed to notice. Maybe no one cared. Cherry made it sound so fun and glamorous on-line, but up close, I thought it was ugly. All those parts she left out.

I tried to shake off those poisonous feelings and said, "Hey, I brought you something." Carlotta admired the perfectly ripe avocado. It filled her hand. The outside was dark and felt like reptile skin. She handled it gently, encouraging it, evaluating it. No squishy bruise spots, no hard resistance, just an even balance between the state of being firm and the state of yielding.

"Good enough for you?" I smiled.

Carlotta grinned back. Her dark eyes swallowed me up. She flicked open her switchblade and pressed a solid line around the fruit, lengthwise. The two parts fell away from each other, one with a smooth hole where the pit had rested and the other with the round brown seed rising out like an unseeing eye. She stabbed the seed and expertly flicked it out. She waved it around on the end of her knife.

"Simone, you sure can pick them." We admired the flawless pale green and yellow insides. She held the knife so I could pull off the slimy pit. Then she scooped out the flesh in wedges, eating it right off the blade. Her long fingers were painted red at the tips. Silver rings flashed as she swiveled the fruit to scrape out the last bit of green. I watched the rippling movement of tendons and ligaments from her wrist, up her shapely brown arms to her broad shoulders. Her black hair danced over flatness, where breasts should've grown. Up and up I followed, over that despised lump which bobbed each time she swallowed. All the way to her mouth.

Carlotta's lips were full and sexy. I watched them move and nothing else mattered. Not Cherry, ditching me and hooring around town. Not school, and failing out. Or money, and how I had none. Or a job, which I needed. The Suits reading their papers and checking their stocks didn't count, and neither did the Security Guard, who was giving us the evil eye, getting ready to come and kick me out of the fountain and right out of the corporate world. There was only Carlotta's mouth and the sucking, mashing, and swallowing of my avocado. She tossed the empty peels at me.

"You're lookin' at me like I'm Mama's tortilla, hot off the pan. You girls always trying to make me a lezzie, but you know I got my boyfriend now. *Mira*, sometimes you and your *chicas* got more manness than my Pretty Boi."

I laughed.

"Thanks, Simone." Carlotta stood up from the fountain and collected her things. "I gotta check the library. You coming?"

But I was lighting up a smoke and stretching out on the grass with my feet up on the ledge she just vacated. I was thinking about putting my pants back on.

She leaned over and said, "Well, are you coming to class at least?"

"Yeah, yeah. See ya in ten."

"Ciao."

I rolled over on my belly and watched her saunter away in those crazy shoes, swinging that miniskirt like nobody else could.

The avocado peels curled and dried in my hand.

Cherry's Blog: Most Recent Entry
Wednesday, June 4 8:53 PM

Who knows how to cover hickeys with foundation?! I tried everything, but it still looks like I had a date with a vampire. Vampire V.
☺ He said he wanted everyone to know I'm "Taken." He's such a
softie! He was even a little jealous about the web site job. Cute,
eh? I would love to make money stripping only for him, but life's not
fair, is it? So anyways, tonight's our big audition at the Porno Palace
web site. Simone, if you're reading this you should be getting ready.
Better yet, call me! Where are you? You better not make me do this
alone! Meet me at the diner next door to the place at midnight, got
it? I'll be the sexy redhead sipping coffee.

   XOX I can't wait to not be broke. I need this job sooo bad.

mOsH
Pit

Mood: Excited and Edgy
Music: The Distillers

chapter thirteen:

Our New Job

"How did you hear about our company?"

Douglas peered down at us through expensive, wire frame glasses. He smoothed his Italian suit and sniffed with boredom. He tapped his manicured fingers on the counter between us while Brian, his partner in business and life, smiled encouragingly from somewhere near Douglas' right shoulder.

"Oh, personal recommendation. You have quite a reputation with every homeless kid with really low self-esteem in the city." Cherry smiled saccharine into his surprised face. "Just joking. Some guy gave me your card at a club we go to. I'm Cherry and this is my obedient slave. We're just dying to try out for your new Wrestleshemania Web site. Really."

Douglas recovered quickly. Being sassed must've been an occupational hazard, since he employed underage girls to roll around in pink gymnastic leotards on his ever-expanding internet porn site. He said, "Then I'm sure you are aware of our hair policy. Either you wear a wig," he said to me directly, "or you come back when that hair is grown out." He wrinkled his nose, as if my Mohawk smelled bad. Like he thought it was writhing with lice or something.

"She'll be wearing a cute blue bob," said Cherry. She pulled it out of her bag and twirled it around on her fingers. "That okay?"

"Yes, well . . . we'd prefer a hair color found in nature," said Douglas. "But it just so happens we have a rather urgent opening. You'll stay tonight and do a two-hour trial training shift for which you will not be paid. I repeat, for which you will NOT be paid. We give you the costume tonight if you are offered the position. You will take your costume home and launder it carefully, and you will bring it to each and every shift you are given."

Brian nodded vigorously.

"You can get changed in the ladies' room back there, and find your way to Room Four. Questions?" Douglas swooped his hands to indicate the shabby doorway partially covered by a long piece of cheap red fabric and strings of plastic beads that clinked together when you walked through them.

"Charmed, I'm sure." Cherry trotted off and I followed behind haltingly, as though my invisible leash was snagged somewhere along on the carpet.

The first time I ever heard about porno Web sites was from a couple of girls who panhandled near our school. Emily, this cute girl with a Chelsea, told us the deal. She didn't have a cushy computer at home with her own web cam, so she started working here. She said basically you just sit around in some theme room, like a dungeon or a weight room or a little girl's pink bedroom, bored out of your tree forever, waiting for the computer monitor in your room to beep. When this happens, it means some on-line guy clicked your special room just to see you. The video camera in your room starts recording and sends a live feed to the Web site. So when it beeps you have to leap into character and start the action. Every time a new person logs onto your room you hear another beep and the longer you keep them interested and watching from their computer somewhere in Idaho or Nebraska or wherever, the more money gets racked up on their credit card and the more moolah Douglas and Brian make. We'd get paid the same amount, no matter who was watching. Twelve bucks an hour. More than you make at McCrappers, that's for sure.

"What are you doing in there? A high colonic?!" Cherry banged on the door of my bathroom stall. "Hurry up."

I tugged and jumped, tried to stretch the ridiculous outfit over all the parts it was supposed to cover and tippy-toed over to the mirror. I didn't want to ruin the sock feet of my nice new leos. Getting the wig on was tricky. I had to rinse the glue out of my hair in order to fit anything on my head, and that made a huge mess in the rust-stained sink. I rubbed my hair with paper towels to dry it, then fought to get it all underneath the wig netting. I had a hard time getting the thing on properly, but when I finished I looked really different.

"What do you think?" I added more eyeliner and put Cherry's shiny lip gloss all over my lips.

Cherry looked at my reflection and didn't say anything at first. She readjusted the wig, fluffed it up a bit. "You look hot," she said, finally. She looked at me so intensely, I thought she might kiss me for real. I smiled and she smiled back and an electrifying warmth rolled over us, zapped between us, held us together. It was a heat that had been missing for some time. Since that time in the mosh pit, I realized. It was a perfect, wordless moment and probably the last time we'd ever share one, though I didn't know it then. And as suddenly as it bloomed, our tangled emotions faded and dropped, a ghost fleeing the scene of the crime. We left the girls' bathroom and headed down the cold hallway to Room Four.

"Cherry? Are you nervous?"

"Get real, Simone. Nice decor."

Room Four was gray and ugly and awful. As far as theme rooms go, Room Four was kind of a nothing room that was maybe undergoing renovations or something. No color and no real furniture. Only the computer monitor and the video camera all set up. We sat around and Cherry did her nails and I tried to not throw up. I read a wrestling magazine to get some moves down pat. Cherry didn't want to practice so that was that.

"My frigging nails are still wet! God, we're not getting nominated for Oscars or anything, you know."

Cherry didn't want to talk about her new friends or her new habits either.

"What, you want us to go to couples' counseling or something? There's no problem except you're moody and no fun. You wanna hang with me, then stop being so judgmental. How's that for processing?"

"Cherry, do you miss school?"

"Right," she said, sarcastically.

I guess I'd meant, *Do you miss me?* But she still saw me. No one else from our gang came out to her parties, and she never asked about them, either. It was *me* that missed *her*. I missed her at school and I missed her each night as I watched the recognizable traits, the Cherry I knew, shrink smaller and harder and get lost in the brittle meanness that was her massive drug cocktail.

So, instead of talking about what was going on in her life, in her demented spiraling disaster of a life (she didn't see it that way at all!), we sat around and every now and then Douglas or Brian came around and rapped on the door or just plain opened it up to see what we were up to, I guess. They could've just peeped through the video monitor, of course, but I guess they wanted us to know that we were supposed to be doing something.

Beep.

Cherry looked up casually as if she were about to check her clothes in the dryer at some laundromat.

I started to throw up. All those nice pancakes I'd eaten at the diner, just before. It actually came all the way up my

93

throat and I could taste a little of it at the back of my mouth, but then Cherry gave me that look and I swallowed it back down. She grabbed my arm and pulled me onto the floor which, I might add, was cold, crappy cement covered by a lousy wool army blanket for comfort. Maybe I fainted. I'm not really sure. All I know is I was suddenly lying across Cherry's legs and looking up at her while she seduced the anonymous fellow (as it turned out, Douglas and Brian!) with her quick wit and flirtatious repartee. Apparently they couldn't really hear her but I watched from underneath as her chin moved when she talked and kissed the camera.

It reminded me of something pretty wacky she did when we were on mushrooms once. She lay on my bed with her head hanging over the edge so that it hung back and her chin was up in the air. She put a pair of my army pants around her face covering her upside-down nose and drew eyes and nose holes on the front part of her chin. Then she started talking as "Mr. Chinigin" and even if it sounds moronic it was actually hilarious and I almost peed myself.

So this is what I was thinking about, and of course I started snorting up a storm, and of course Cherry didn't like that and tried to strangle me while talking about Mr. Nobody's big hard package, and of course Douglas and Brian barged right in to tell us we were two seconds away from getting thrown out so we had better smarten up.

"You are dreadfully lucky that this is a dress rehearsal of sorts. Brian and myself are simulating a real paying customer." That's what Douglas said. *Simulating.*

Brian had yet to open his mouth and for that reason I thought he was nicer than Douglas. But Cherry said, "Just 'cause someone's quiet doesn't mean they're not a bloody mean bastard."

So for the rest of our trial shift I didn't do too much. Mostly I just let Cherry throw me around, or put me in a half nelson, or suffocate me by sitting on my head. Boy, they liked that one all right! Douglas said they'd pick that still shot to go on our advertising lobby web page. *If* we got hired, that is.

By two thirty a.m. I was starving. I couldn't focus anymore. My leotards were all saggy in the crotch and my feet were too hot and itchy, but that's when Douglas said the big rush started, when all those straight male losers got home from the bar, trashed and lonely. Even Cherry was a bit worn out and she'd been snuffling up a good bag of coke, courtesy of Vincent, when the screen was dead.

She said, "Put some effort in, for chrissakes."

I said, "I'm hungry."

"You just ate a million pancakes at the diner!"

"Well, I'm hungry again. You must be starved." Cherry chain-smoked and drank bottomless cups of coffee with sugar. She hardly ever ate. At the diner I told her she was too skinny so she'd grabbed a piece of my toast, taken a huge bite. When she went to the can I'd found the nasty crumpled-up napkin with partly chewed bread hidden in there, still warm from her mouth.

"Cry me a river," she said. "You've been lying around all night."

"Okay, Cherry. If I pin you for real, you buy breakfast. Deal?"

"Breakfast? We're going to that hip hop After Hours. I'm meeting Vincent. You pin me, I'll buy you a beer."

I hated Vincent more than ever but hanging with Lucette almost made up for it. I smiled for Big Brother and sailed right into a whopping su-flex, rolled Cherry around, and pulled her hair. We grunted and struggled and I used the strength of my legs to pry hers apart and keep her where I wanted her. Then I just put the weight of my body right over her shoulders so there was no way she was going anywhere. Then I did the nastiest stunt I could think up for a glorious finish. I twisted my torso dramatically back and forth in front of her so my boobs actually smacked her face to the left and then the right and so on.

The monitor started beeping like there was no tomorrow and that's when we knew for sure that those cheap, pervy, fags were no longer "simulating" customers. Actual real paying customers were actually already logged on to us and we were not actually getting paid yet. Then Cherry bit me you-know-where and we rolled around arguing for a bit and then, thank Christ, our time was over, and Douglas told us we were hired and handed us a schedule, and Cherry had to buy me a beer after all.

At the After Hours, however, Cherry admitted she was totally broke. She said she forgot her wallet at home, so I bought us beers while she made trips around the place searching for Vincent, who never showed. Every few minutes she took a neurotic peep at her cell to see if he had called, to see what time it was now, and if it was too soon to try phoning him again. "I bet he's with that blonde slut who was all over him last night," she snarled.

I worried about Lucette, hoped whoever he was with was being nice to her, at least.

"That fucking liar said he'd be here," she yelled, a half hour later.

"Yeah. He must be the first man to break a promise in the history of dating."

"Shut up," she snapped.

"Very original," I said. "Him for being a fuck up and you for taking it out on your loyal friend here. I told you he was bad news." My attitude only fueled her outrage. Cherry cursed. She hexed him. She asked everybody if he'd been there, when he'd left, when he was coming back. She promised to tell him off, listed his cardinal sins, practiced the scene she'd make when she saw him next, and I was secretly cheered by the thought that her sudden romance might end as quickly. I thought we'd go back to being the dynamic duo we'd always been. I was so naïve.

"Let's take off," I said. "Let's just go some place else. Forget about him."

She had a calculated look on her face. "Okay, let's go down to that other party. The Biker Boozecan. Maybe he's there."

"No way, Cherry. You're like totally stalking the guy."

I noticed the guys Vincent hung with were smirking and rolling their eyes at her behind her back. They definitely knew where he was and who he was with, and even though I thought I might ultimately profit from the situation, I was embarrassed for her.

"Let's go to Hardcore Hank's. We can buy some beers off him," I said.

"Yeah, right. With what money, Simone? Vincent's supposed to pay me back tonight."

"You gave money to Vincent?"

Frank's money.

"Don't ask, and don't start in on me," she said. "He needed to pay back some dude in order to get the next batch to sell, or he'd never make any money."

She lied about her wallet!

I bit back all the things I wanted to hurl at her, at him, at Frank. "You gave money to Vincent?"

"Forget about it," she said and sipped her beer. But how could I? How could she?!

Cherry said, "Let's talk about our brilliant career moves as future porn stars. I can't believe we have to wait until Friday to get paid."

"Guess I have to think up a stage name," I said. "Who are you going to be?"

"Duh. I already have the ultimate porn name. Why mess with perfection?"

I wasn't sure if it was absolute egotism on her part or if she really thought none of this would ever come back to haunt her later in life. Say, if she cleaned up her act and ran for political office or wanted to lead a Girl Guide troupe or something.

Her teeth were clenched and that tiny cheek tremor betrayed her bad nerves. She had no money so she couldn't buy outright. The other guys were a bit wary of her now, since she was considered one of Vincent's girls. Clearly that status was a bit in question at the moment. But still, she'd been having bad luck, trying to flirt for free lines. Unless some Big Dude wanted to pick a fight with him directly or a good natured eunuch arrived with some hits for her, she was shit outta luck.

When I tried to buy her one last beer, she asked for the money instead. "Lend me twenty?"

"Cherry, that's all I have."

"Ten?" She was biting her lip and holding her breath, biting so that the bottom lip went white and tiny droplets of blood started to pool up under her shining teeth.

I handed it to her. What else could I do? She tore off to the back, where she'd been feverishly watching the activity. And what do you know? Sure enough, some Big Dude, some rival dealer Hip Hop Daddy, chatted her up and before long they were off in the corner with his friends, snorting lines. He was rubbing her back, his big hand resting on the back of her neck. Somebody passed around a pipe.

I sat on a stool by the speakers, chillin'. My wrestling bruises hadn't surfaced yet and *Missy Elliot* was telling it like it is. I nodded to the beat, tried to lap up her attitude. I let myself go, exhaled anxieties, blew them into the air, and sent that part of myself that felt horror or fear or premonition way up high, to where the bare pipes rode the ceiling and pushed their way through the drywall, into other secret parts of the building I knew nothing about. The beer tasted like shite but it brought a softening to my joints, a loosening that I needed in order to drift. To be a drifter.

I watched Cherry, over in the middle of the knot of men. She was miming some of our wrestling moves, animating a story for them. She was advertising the Web site already, ready to sign autographs and score more drugs. Typical. She turned and pointed to me, still blabbing away. The men stared confidently. They took in my clothes, my flaccid hawk and piercings, and I knew that I was part of their consideration now, and that I hadn't been before. For the moment I had the starring role in their collective fantasy, probably *Freaky Teen Slut Likes It Rough!* or something. Cherry had lassoed me, was tightening the rope, and sooner or later I'd be pulled into their hairy, macho midst.

Then, out of Nowhere, I had a rather unrelated thought. My porn name was going to be Roxy. I imagined her, this mythical beast, part teenager, part rock star, part Neolithic Priestess. Roxy would wear the electric blue bob and lots of eyeliner. Roxy would be a combination of all the bravest girls I knew.

All the girlfriends I ever wanted to have.

All the women I ever wanted to be.

chapter fourteen:
Going Home

"Why don't you go home? Wear some of your own clothes for a change. And don't forget, we're working Friday night."

Cherry was at party peak, way past listening to me, and on the verge of getting violent if provoked. I was beside myself, fighting off flashbacks of Frank and sick about Vincent having all her money. I glared at everyone near us, fully hostile. The men wanted her to stay. The women couldn't care less. I was desperate for her to come with me but she wouldn't leave. Not before "telling Vincent off"—or so she said. I knew what it was to wait and want for someone, knew she wouldn't be telling him anything she pretended. She had it bad for Vincent, and I knew right then this romance of hers was not going to end any time soon. Even worse, I knew from her own treatment of me that she wouldn't gain back any points by hanging around, hoping for him. Her tenacity was remarkable and it sealed her fate, in a way. Cherry was staying.

She pushed me out the door. I was going "home." What a word for that miserable place. A two-bedroom vault without the dust. The place I visited a couple times a week to change clothes and do laundry. The address I wrote on forms: a number, a street, and a name that only doctors and social workers ever used. In fact, I'd hardly been there since the night of the Cuntagion show.

The Tomb.

I walked. I walked away from Cherry and that cracked-out madness, walked briskly with fear and loathing fueling me. Pennies jingled in my pocket. Seventeen pennies, to be precise. One for each of my humid, mind-baking summers. I cut through alleys and parks, stole sips from a hundred different water fountains, watched the world wake up. I was immune to its magic. I neared the market but it was way too early to run into people I knew. Unless they were just stumbling home, like me. Shopkeepers were opening up, unloading fresh produce by the crate. Dirty trucks delivered bread from a bakery. One van had boxes of long silvery fish, embedded in ice. Open mouths, dead eyes, pointed right at me. A man wearing a bloody apron carried a whole goat, skinned and frozen, to the butcher's across the street.

Murder!

I was coming down big time. The world was evil, and everything sucked. The Pepper Patio, where we liked to drink watered-down draft beer and eat stale pretzels, was locked up and the shades drawn. An old woman slept on the doorstep, her hand on the wheel of a shopping cart filled with newspapers and other precious belongings. I walked past Hank's place. There were cars parked on the tiny front lawn and three motorcycles up by the side door. A big guy I didn't recognize was tranced out, sitting in a plastic lawn chair by the stoop. I didn't feel like dealing with strangers, so I headed to Punker Park instead.

I recognized some kids over by the bench. They were all conked out in a nest of their knapsacks and sleeping bags. I'd see them at shows sometimes, and out on the street. There was one older boy, two girls, and two androgynous waifs. Dirt-smudged. Sleeping. A baby pit bull stretched out in the very center. Orphaned. I wanted to fall down, to curl up with them, to belong. To be part of a pack, to feel their warmth. To pretend I wasn't alone. I missed Lucette. And as I stood there hesitating, the oldest boy opened one neutral eye. I nodded at him. Kept walking.

I went past quietly and picked my favorite tree on the other side, over by the kiddie pool. I undid my boots, pulled them off, rubbed the sock fluff out from my sweaty toes, rinsed my feet in the water. I tied my boots together with the laces, laid them down flat, side by side, and put my work bag with the leotard and blue wig on top, to make a pillow. Then I crashed.

Time travel.

That's how it felt the millisecond before waking. There was the void I'd fallen into, and then there was suction. A pulling and a stirring and then there was light. The feeling that someone was watching me. I opened my eyes. It was really fucking bright out. I couldn't see shit. Little kids were running and screaming in the tiny wading pool. When my eyes adjusted, I noticed the street kids were gone. I saw a little girl who looked like one of Carlotta's twin sisters when they were toddlers. She had big dark eyes and little drippy pigtails sticking out on the sides. Her mom was sitting on a bench nearby, this Goth chick who used to go to our school. She was all in black, holding a black umbrella to keep the mid-morning sun off her skin. I never really knew her or anything, but we were both in the same terrible grade nine math class.

"Hey," I croaked. My mouth was really dry. I cleared my throat horribly.

She smiled.

"Nice shirt." I pointed to her *Nine Inch Nails* tee. "Go to the show?"

"No. I was busy having her. Can't really go to a concert when you're having contractions and shit. My boyfriend got it for me."

Whoops. Remove tongue piercing, insert combat boot.

"She's a cutie," I said.

The kid was stamping around and humming some funny little-kid noises and splooshing water around with her feet.

"Thanks. She's my life."

It was kind of funny to see her in a maternal light, what with her rubber spiked collar, shredded fishnets, and giant ass

104

party boots. She smiled so wide, I wondered if her *Kiss Me Deadly* lipstick would crack and peel right off. There was a huge bag attached to the stroller contraption crammed with animal crackers and diapers and little storybooks and plastic toys in primary colors. They'd look strange in her pale hands with the ultra long black nails.

"How's school?" she said. "Going to Prom?"

"No way," I said. "You're not missing anything, believe me."

I didn't mention that Cherry dropped out and I might as well have. That I was failing. That things seemed to be closing in, not just for Cherry, as was my original concern, but for me as well. Suddenly I wondered if maybe she *was* missing out. And if I was, too. It bugged me that I couldn't remember her name but I was too embarrassed to ask, so I took off. I walked slower in the last stretch of the way. I was really tired.

My mom always said she was too young when she had me, but she was already done high school. She got a special graduation gift from my old man, if you know what I mean. I guess she was pretty mortified about it all. She's big on manners.

Outside The Tomb I stalled, but that was dumb. I gave myself a little pep talk, like, *no worries, it won't be like that other time, everything's cool.* I opened the door with my key. It was really quiet, as usual. It smelled like cleaner.

Artificial lemony scent.

I could hear the clock ticking from the kitchen at the end of the hall.

"Mom?" I closed the door behind me and dropped my bag. "Are you home?"

I peeked in her bedroom but nobody was there. The bed was made. So perfect you could bounce a penny off it.

All seventeen of them.

Everything was dusted and put in its place, and the blinds were lowered precisely two-thirds of the way down, to block out snoopers and let in a bit of light at the same time. Her slippers were lined up beside the bed with the heel parts facing out, ready for someone to slide their feet right in there. I backed out and closed the door behind me.

The bathroom was spotless.

Exhale.

I was already halfway in the kitchen when I noticed her sitting at the table looking at her photo album. She was touching the pictures lightly and turning the pages. She was telling herself all those stories she made up for each picture. The one where she's dressed up and going on a date with my father. The one where she's dancing with him at their graduation. The corsage he planted on her tiny wrist. The fortune that came in her cookie that night.

"Mom?"

I didn't want to scare her, but she was in her own world so much of the time that she didn't always remember that I was supposed to be living there, too. As much as I hated being home, every time I walked in and saw her sitting there I'd die a new death. *Guilt-inflicted gun wounds. Slashed wrists. Seven-story free fall.*

I could almost hear her words. Her lips were moving and her fingers moved around the photos. Sometimes she stopped talking and cocked her head like she was listening to someone talk back to her. She nodded and smiled to Mr. Nobody.

"Mom!"

She turned suddenly and looked at me like a stranger. She clutched the album to her chest.

"Mom, it's me. Simone. I'm on page nine. Remember? Have a look."

"You're not my Simone. Look at your filthy hair. Look at those slacks! No, no, no. You can't be in my book."

She placed a chair between us.

I sat down in the corner away from her, hangover in full gear. My eyes were hot and bulgy, like two fried eggs, and my stomach was queasy. I was in no mood for this rigmarole.

"Where's Pamela, Mom? Did she come and give you your pills today?"

No response.

"Do I have any messages? Telephone calls?"

Nothing.

"Your hair looks pretty, Mom. Did you set the curlers yourself?"

She patted it self-consciously and admired her reflection in the toaster.

"Of course I do my own hair! A lady always does her own curls. She just makes it look as though it's professional."

She relaxed her shoulders a bit and let the book rest on the kitchen table. "You girls today could take a few lessons in style and fashion."

That made me smile.

"Did you do your own color rinse, too?"

107

"Color? I never colored my hair in my life! Did Pamela tell you that? It's a vicious rumor. I've always been a blonde. Since I was a little girl."

Me and Miss Clairol knew all about mom's blonde hair.

Summer Wheat Sheaf No.126.

"Would you like to look at my pictures?"

"Okay, Mom. But only for a minute. I have to lie down."

"Oh, yes."

And she started back at the first page, telling me for the millionth time the stories I already knew by heart.

Cherry's Blog: Most Recent Entry

Friday, June 6 4:16 PM

At this wacked cyber café place downtown weird using a brand new computer. On a bit of a run as they say. Waiting for my man. What's left of him, after I practically ripped his head off the other day for standing me up. He was so sorry you bettah believe it, gave me lots of treats to make it up. Met some totally new peops crashed at their place downtown. Cool murals all over the wall inside this place. Found a big art book cool pictures. Learning lots. Way more than at school. Hey is it really Friday holy shit I had no idea. Gotta get some sleep. Been a blurr. Simone I gotta talk to you. So we're working later, right? I think at like eleven or something. We get paid tonight, right? Because I really really need money and maybe you can lend me some? So guess I'll call The Tomb. My phone's fucked, battery died. I have to steal some quarters right after I run out on the puter nerds here. Why don't you ever post? This is practically our only means of communication now! Fucking Luddite.

Mood: Wired, need Weed

Music: Assholes are playing some barfy easy rock. Phil fucking Collins!

chapter fifteen

The Tomb

I stared at myself in the mirror. The bathroom door was locked. The faucets were polished. The porcelain was spotless. I felt the weight of the razor in my hand.

I thought terrible thoughts.

Then I shook the can and pressed out the thick foam and smothered the sides of my head with the stuff. I half-filled the sink with hot water and swished the razor around in the basin.

Swish drip drip.

The electric feel of sharp metal on skin. I made long deliberate strokes and then *swish drip drip.* More scrapes along the surface and I smiled at myself, loving this sexy ritual, this striptease. More face. It was all about having more face.

Doing the back part was harder. I held a small mirror up and looked into it and then back into the reflection from the bathroom cabinet. Even now, after tons of practice, I still failed the hand-eye coordination test with the razor moving up and away instead of down, firmly, and along the nape of the neck. Mistakes got made and were marked by the trails of long green tufts, falling soft and slow, down to white tiles beside my feet.

In the shower I discovered more of these betrayed locks. My hands moved through wet hair with shampoo and later with slippery conditioner, and with each pull I felt the loosening of small knotted clumps. I rubbed my hands together quickly to ball them up and flicked the hairballs over the top of the shower curtain.

If I wasn't more careful I'd end up with a Nohawk.

I took a fresh blade and shook the can again. I ran my fingers over the stubble between my legs. I liked to be smooth and clean. Freshly and completely shaved.

My skin was cooler now. I smelled like fruity shampoo and soap and I was brand new. Only one smallish cut on the left side of my head. I slapped a Band-Aid on it and padded down the hall.

I closed and locked my bedroom door. White painted walls met a white painted ceiling. A geometric patterned, blue rug lay underneath. In one corner, my dusty electric bass stared back at me, a petulant stranger. A wobbly, child-sized desk glared from the opposite corner, weighted by an avalanche of textbooks and binders. The bed. Shiny polyester bedspread. Two matching throw pillows. I lay on the narrow mattress and looked up at the ceiling. The light fixture, that central hub, was pure seventies disaster. The glow-in-the-dark, Milky Way stickers chased one another around the room, mostly up there on the ceiling. Some dribbled down the walls a bit.

I rubbed my smooth legs against each other and a long ago memory of Carol Thompson ambushed me. Carol and her gorgeous blonde hair. Carol's flesh on mine during a one-time make-out session under the basement stairs at school, cut short by Fate in the guise of an old janitor. I hadn't seen Carol in a long time. Did she still exist? I touched my own skin. Carol's face faded.

Clocks ticked in The Tomb. Time passed. Silk, satin, and after, plain polyester.

Later, I thought that the silence was most unnerving. People often say they'd give anything for a bit of quiet. But lying there on that—my—single bed I knew there were worse things than movement and chaos, energy and confusion. Silence was and always would be insatiable. I felt him close in, not breathing, hovering just above me. This quiet monster crept into my bones and, like a winter chill, spread himself along pathways of veins and arteries, strands of nerve and hair follicles, until all joints seized up and a stiffness took over my whole being.

Silence fed on my insides, there in The Tomb.

I had hours to kill before work.

And all this nothingness threatened to seal me in forever.

Cherry's Blog: Most Recent Entry
Tuesday, June 10 2:53 PM

Went to some dance party last night instead of the usual bar. Took a break from my regular mix and did some killer MDMA with V. I forgot how much I love that shit! Everything rises up inside you and blends with the sounds, the lights. V. didn't want to dance but then how could he not when everyone in the place was? Everyone was feeling it, no fights, just friendly smiles and me and V. kissing on the dance floor forever. It felt like my insides, like ME, was liquid smoke or something that could ooze right through the sensitive micro layers of my skin and through V.'s skin, so that I could be inside him and he in me. Every bit of our skin that touched, vaporized, and we stared into each others' giant eyes and dripped slow, like honey. Dreamy Fun, like the world has love and is a good place after all.

V. left Lucette with his cousin so we stopped by to pick her up on our way back to V.'s place this morning. How can they be related?! His cousin is some creepy guy with major zits and greasy hair, wearing track pants and no shirt. Gross. They kept talking and drinking and then V. didn't feel like driving home. We popped some valium to soften the crash but it was kinda too late for me. Felt like crap then V. tossed me a bag before crashing (we've been up four days). I can't believe he was holding out on me, but I guess that just proves how generous he is and how he's weakened by my powers of seduction. Now I'm wired and can't sleep! Hope that freaky guy doesn't wake up before V. I don't wanna talk to him. But he has a nice computer ☺

Mood: High Alert, Code Red

Music: None.Because I can't figure out how to turn his stereo on. Fuck!

chapter sixteen

Man To Man

Happy hour. That's what the big sign says in the window of the bar we were at. Only somebody crossed out the first "H" and wrote in "CR."

Crappy Hour.

Hardcore Hank was threatening the bartender with a pool cue 'coz he thought the guy was holding out on us.

"I know you have those little peanuts somewhere. Fuck."

"We're out, man. It's pretzels or nothin'. You want pretzels or you want nothin'?" He rubbed the dishtowel over his shaved head and yawned with the pool cue right under his chin, taking little pokes at the top of his T-shirt.

"Forget it. I hate pretzels." Hank tossed a few fake punches then paraded around, checking each table for any sign of the goddamn peanuts.

I was sitting on a stool at the bar. I swigged my beer. The one Hank bought me. I was thinking about Cherry, missing in action. Not a word from her since work on Friday. Her phone was dead. Her mother knew dick, hadn't seen her since some huge fight they'd had last week, and wasn't interested in finding her yet. There were her sporadic blog updates. I could comment on them, but it wasn't the same thing as talking to her.

Cherry was gone, tripping some path that spiraled wildly, dancing with danger in the perfect after-school special. One of those three-part series where they introduce a new character to kill off in the end. One that gets you feeling pretty badly about partying for a while. But it's never a character you couldn't live without. That's how everyone else seemed to see Cherry, too. A write-off.

"Ever heard the expression 'Pick yer battles?'" Hank looked me in the eye and rubbed the spot under his lower lip, where he was growing some kind of goatee. I noticed the dirt and bicycle grease caked under his thumbnail and smudged on the back of his hand.

"Would you shut up about the peanuts already?" I said. "Gawd."

He kept rubbing that spot and looking right at me. "I'm over the peanuts now. I'm not talking about the peanuts. I'm talking about that walking zombie. Your freaked-out friend."

"Who? Cherry?"

"Yeah, you've got that depressed missionary look on your face again. Or should I say, 'still.'" Figured you're crying in your beer over that screwed-up broad. Figured maybe I'd try to think of some friendly advice for you, before you drive yourself crazy and I have to visit you in some mental ward where they'll make you grow your hair out and start wearing nylons and shit."

"What are you trying to say?"

"You're not the only one who cares about her, you know," he said. "Look around you! Not here in the bar, ya goof. Especially not here. She owes a lot of them money. Other folks are rooting for Cherry. But Cherry's not. Not yet, any-ways. Know what I mean?"

"Fuck, no." I swigged my beer. I was drumming on the bar with my other hand.

"Relax, would you? I'm just trying to let you know. I see what's going on and I know what it's like to watch somebody who's so great turn themselves into a fucking pincushion or a glue bag or whatever. It sucks. But you can't save nuthin' that doesn't want to be saved."

He took a long gulp from the bottle. "Like you can try to save a whale but probably not a lemming."

"So Cherry's a lemming." Sarcasm dribbled down my chin and left wet marks on my favorite *Motorhead* shirt.

"Exactly! Get it?" Hank leaned back and cracked his neck on both sides, then ran those dirty fingers through his orange 'hawk. He grabbed my shoulder and roughed it up a bit. "Maybe—and I fucking hope this is the case—just maybe she'll have herself a big scare and get out in time. Right now she can't see for shit. Been there myself. Had a few close calls. Not on crack, mind you. Yep, I'm lucky to be here today, as a matter of fact. And I still have my good looks, too." He smiled and stuck the very tip of his tongue out at me from the hole where his broken canine used to be.

"Hank," I said. I smiled back at him because I knew he was trying to cheer me up, but inside I just felt sicker. A thousand redheads charged happily over the cliff in my mind.

He said, "It's fucking sad. Don't get me wrong. It kills me. She's smart and gutsy. Sexy as hell. But you and I can't get her out of this. I tried talkin' some sense into her but she won't listen. Every time I see her I tell her what a loser creep Vincent is. I says to her, 'Since when does the sun shine out of that junkie's asshole?' She told me to go—well, never mind. She thinks I'm jealous, right? You know we had a little thing a while ago. Before Vincent came around."

I guess I looked surprised because Hank started to backtrack.

"Hey, I thought you knew. She said there was nothing going on between you two. I mean, fuck. I know how you feel about her, but I thought that was all over. Don't hate me. Eh? It's hard to say no."

I shook my head. I wished he'd shut right up. But that wasn't one of Hank's strong suits, shutting up when he's already blabbed too much. I thought of all those times we crashed at his place and she sent me out to get smokes or more booze in the middle of the night.

"Well, if it makes you feel any better, she stole my fucking stereo. Pawned it while I was still passed out the other day.

Invited Fuckface Vincent over and they partied in my house while I was snoring away upstairs. Shit."

Hank stirred his finger in the little pile of ripped-up beer bottle labels that I'd been meticulously peeling and scraping during our man to man talk.

"They left their fucking pipes right there on the carpet. It was smoldering when I came down and there they were. Could've burnt the whole place down."

I could hardly hear him over the music. He was grinding his teeth. I watched a little muscle twitch in his cheek on one side. I figured I knew how ugly the picture was in his mind. I'd seen enough myself, and I knew how it sickened me to witness, to remember. A quiet feeling settled over us. Our worry for her and our hurts and the nameless outrage we felt gelled into some kind of silent fraternity while we sipped our beer.

"Hank, listen." I felt weird doing it but I tried to kind of rub or pat his arm a bit, but I ended up doing it too hard and knocked his hand so his beer bottle went shooting across the little counter and down to smash on the service side of the floor.

"Shit." The bartender glared over at me and pointedly took out a little broom and matching dustpan from a hidden cupboard while the other patrons whistled and hooted. "Sorry," I said. "I'm a fuck-up."

"No worries, Simone. Last night that guy was opening bottles with his teeth and spitting the caps at everyone. Talk about manners."

"Hank, I'm not mad at you," I said.

"Bullshit. You hate my guts."

"Okay, I'm pissed but I can't really blame you. Only you should've told me." This part was hard to say. "She was never my real girlfriend. Well, maybe for a while. But she only wanted me if no one else was around. I guess I pretended it was all right. Well, I kept hoping, you know. That she'd change her mind about all that. But, no. She always said if I was a boy I'd be perfect. Well, I'm not a fucking boy, am I? I don't want to be one, either."

I finally looked up and met his gaze. "But if I was a guy, Hank, you never would've had a chance." I laughed a bit because it felt strange but good to talk about it out loud for once. "And anyways, your stereo fucking sucked."

Hank laughed, too. The bartender slid two more beers our way and we clinked them together.

"Let it go. Time to move on," he said. "And if rumors serve me right, I think there might be a certain beautiful blonde in the wings." He winked at me lasciviously.

I got a juicy picture of Carol in mind and when I snapped out of it, I noticed he was still in his own dreamland haze.

"Oh, no," I said to him. "Get your own girl. Carol's mine. I saw her first!"

Hank laughed and rubbed his dirty knuckles on the top of my head. He raised his bottle and said, "Here's to the red-haired vixen; may she clean up her act and become worthy of our admiration once again!"

Hank's the king of making toasts.

"Here's to Casanova, punkly Prince Charming," I said. "May your next conquest not steal any of your appliances."

"And here's to Sister Carpet Muncher, patron saint of female genitalia. May your faith and spiritual strength guide you forward and may you henceforth always preach to the converted!"

"Hank, you're so gross!"

And so we drank to that.

So now I'm at V.'s place using his amazing laptop. Hard to get used to the tiny keys. They're so sensitive. I love watching him sleep. He's gorgeous. Actually I got a bit bored and the dog was whining but I couldn't wake him up no matter what I tried. Believe me I thought of almost everything! Fucking dog just pissed over by the door, all over the place. Stupid mutt! I wish he'd get rid of it. So V. has a bachelor pad in an undisclosed location (not allowed to say!). Lots of locks on the door. I started laughing and said how paranoid was he? and he shut the door, did all the locks up slowly, and then held my face in his hand, pretty hard, and said "don't ever call me paranoid, got that?" Well, sorry!

Anyways, it's all white walls and ceiling. There's a nice old-fashioned tub, the kind with feet. So I wanted to have a bubble bath when we got here (pretty high!) but can you believe he doesn't have any? I used the last squirt of dish detergent and now my cooch is itchy. Figures. Then we crashed and that was like yesterday? Or sometime. Hey you should visit our official website, where me and Simone (or should I say Roxy) take it off and throw each other around! Click here to PornoPalace.com slash Wrestleshemania and we're the hottest chicks on the site. Don't blame me if you end up paying to peek. It's worth it and otherwise we'll both starve and it'll be All Your Fault.

So, back to V.'s room. It's pretty bare in here. Except for the big TV, DVD, XBOX, that sort of guy stuff. Not many books. Lots of pornos, though. Stupid big-boobed chicks. Looks pretty boring. All plastic, no soul. I found the tapes when I was looking for some paper to write down a poem that was wanting to sing itself out of me. I can never write poems on computers. I had to use the greasy back of a pizza box, and it didn't come out the right way at all. Pisser. It was something about how I felt when I woke up and the sun was streaming through one long slit in the black sheet he uses to cover the window. It was a long blade of sunlight cutting into the room, onto this mattress on the floor, and it cut right across me, heating me under the sheet. It felt . . . I don't know. And it reached over and cut across him, too. Only he complained about the light.

Mood: Introspective

Music: The Doors "This is the End" wow V. has some ancient CDs lying around.

chapter seventeen

La Cena con Carlotta y Su Familia

A few days later, I was waiting in the lobby of Carlotta's building for someone to buzz me up. It was a heat wave, and the crowded bus ride at rush hour seemed penance enough for any of my recent transgressions. I wilted in the elevator. But I still smiled when I got to the apartment door, knocked, and it opened a crack. Two sets of skinny arms crossed over two tiny naked chests and four big brown eyes blinked through the chained door at me.

"Simone!" They squealed and fiddled with the locks. "You're in trouble," said one of the girls.

"Yep. Carlotta's mad at you," said the other. "You didn't go to school, right? That's bad, you know."

The girls each grabbed a hand and pulled me into their crowded apartment. Their brother Jorge was playing video games with their cousin Nestor in the living room. Nestor's baby brother, Pablo, slept in a hammock that was strung up in the corner of the room.

"Hey, Simone, long time no see," they said, without looking up.

Carlotta was in the kitchen, getting supper ready. She greeted me with a string of obscenities after telling the twins to cover their ears. "You better get organized with school, *amiga*, or you gonna be in some big-ass trouble."

The twins scampered around the kitchen and pulled on Carlotta's skirt.

"What's for supper?"

One of them planted herself on my lap at the kitchen table. I fluffed up her hair and looked for the birthmark on the back of the neck which was the only way I could tell them apart.

"Aha! Isabelle. So, how's it going?"

"Get off her—it's too hot!" Carlotta rinsed her hands under cold water and splashed her face and neck.

"No, it's not. Jorge put on the fans already."

Isabelle swatted my hand away and swiveled around to talk right in my face.

"Simone, did you get a new earring?" She pulled on the rings in my earlobe and counted them out loud. "How come you have so many?"

"They're decorations. I'm not as gorgeous as you and your sisters so I gotta wear more jewelry to make up for it." I smiled when she patted my head and investigated my Mohawk.

"How come you got a Band-Aid on your head? You would look prettier with nice braids. Want me to do them?"

"Well, no . . . it's okay. I like it this way."

"It's pretty messy." She worked her tiny fingers through the crunchy spokes of hair and sighed with the effort.

Carlotta threw dried beans into a pot with water and salt and a bit of garlic.

"'Lisabeth, get me the rice from the cupboard, and an onion."

"Tie me first." Elisabeth put on one of their mother's aprons and turned so Carlotta could do up the long strings at the back. The bottom dropped well below her knees and the top part moved around when she walked, exposing her nipple here and there like a winking eye. "*Tengo hambre.*"

"Why didn't you ask Jorge to make you something after school?"

"He's busy playing video. And he doesn't do it right."

Carlotta sucked her teeth and yelled into the living room.

"Jorge and Nestor—you're boys, not invalids. Get off your firm, teenaged ass and help make supper."

"We're busy!" one of them yelled. I'm not sure which.

"Too busy to eat?" Carlotta slammed a bag of frozen corn tortillas on the counter.

"We're looking after Pablito. It takes all our concentration." The two boys laughed and kept playing.

127

"Hey, Carlotta!" It was Nestor for sure this time. "Get used to being in the kitchen. You want to be a real woman, right? You know how I like my steak!" He and Jorge laughed loudly.

"*Pendejos!*" Carlotta's eyes glittered dangerously and she stormed into the other room with the chopping knife still in her hand. "Don't push me right now. Don't say nothing to me, *comprendes*? Now shut that *computadora* off and get in there before *I* make women out of you."

The girls and I looked at each other. The game went quiet.

"And don't tell me about women in the kitchen because I see women doing just about everything in this house. Including wiping your skinny asses. *Vamonos.*"

Jorge and Nestor shuffled into the kitchen and we cleared and set the table together. Carlotta came back in, composed, and told us what to chop and where to put it. She was quiet after that and I looked at her carefully. She was tired. Stressed.

Carlotta caught me looking and said, "*Mi tia*'s stupid baby father got a new girlfriend. *Una Canadiense.* So now he has no money for Pablito's daycare. Nothing. She had to take him to work with her when I was at school. Lucky the manager was sick that day because I'm sure he would've loved to fire her for having a baby hidden below the cash register."

"Shit," I said. I realized with a stabbing guilt pang that I had no idea what it was to have little kids depending on me in order to eat or come home or be safe. Weird.

When Carlotta left the room to check on Pablito, Jorge nudged me. "Carlotta finally got her rag, eh?" He laughed behind a piece of lettuce then tossed it into the salad bowl. "Bad mood or what!"

Nestor giggled from the other side of the counter. Then he turned on the radio to a salsa/hip hop station and soon the tension transformed from overheated annoyance to fun. Carlotta danced around the kitchen with Isabelle, and Elisabeth danced with Nestor, standing on the tops of his shoes. Jorge grabbed my hand and tried to lead me but my huge boots got in the way and my whole body felt awkward and oversized.

"*Mira*, Simone. You can look tough and still dance with me." He held my hand firmly and pressed the other one into the small of my back, bringing me closer, squashed flat against him. Part of my Mohawk poked him in the eye when I looked down at my feet.

"Ow!"

"Sorry, Jorge. I . . . I don't dance much." I was caught between wanting to be good at it and wanting to be as far away from all this claustrophobic body contact as possible.

"*Tranquilo*, Jorge. You better get this girl a diaphragm before you take her dancing anywhere." Nestor laughed over his shoulder at us.

"*Si bueno.*" Jorge looked up into my eyes and blushed handsomely. "As soon as I turn sixteen and get my license I gonna take you dancing every Saturday night. If I get a car."

"*Recuerdas, mi amiga es lesbiana, Vato.*" Carlotta laughed and spun Isabelle around and around.

"You can bring your girlfriend, too. If you get one by then." He teased and gracefully twirled me away so I could get my bearings.

"Maybe I can practice first," I said.

"You mean dancing, right?" Jorge winked and I turned red. Carlotta and Nestor laughed loudly.

Nestor danced Elisabeth over to the stove and checked the bubbling pots.

"Hey! It's ready!"

So Elisabeth went to get Pablito and then we all lined up with our plates and Carlotta doled out the fluffy white rice and hot beans and salad, and Nestor put a stack of tortillas, warmed in the toaster oven, out onto the table and we all sat down to eat. I was so hungry, in spite of the hot muggy day, that I couldn't remember the last thing I'd eaten. Hungry for food but also for the feeling in this kitchen at Carlotta's place. For the music on the radio and the smiles around the table and the joking that went on, one to the next. Carlotta used to tease that if their apartment was a little bigger, they'd have adopted me years ago. Most of the time I wish they had.

"Guess you're staying in tonight, eh?" I knew it was dumb to even bring up the idea of a party. I was hoping to not be alone and I knew once Carlotta's mom and her aunt came home there'd be no room for an extra person around here.

Carlotta sucked her teeth and frowned. "I'm staying in until exams are done. You should, too. You can party with Cherry all you want, after." She tapped some warmed-up baby mush onto her wrist to test the temperature, then started spooning blops of it between Pablito's lips. It dripped onto his face. Then he smeared it with his little fists, all over. He kicked his teeny feet and the homemade sockies blurred brightly colored yarn like a cartoon getaway. Carlotta tried to scrape up the goop with the edge of the spoon, and put it back into his wee, gurgling mouth.

I said, "Anyways, I only see her at work these days. She's all Vincent this, Vincent that. Maybe I should scrap the school year altogether," I said.

"Oh, if Cherry jumped off a cliff, would you do that, too?"

"She's your friend, too, you know," I said.

"Yeah, but only in moderation."

Which, as I later thought about it, was a pretty funny phrase to use under the circumstances.

"Since when are you pissed at Cherry?" I asked her. They sure got along well enough when that free coke bag materialized.

"'Sabelle, 'Sabeth, cover your ears." The twins did, and kept chewing on salad and tortilla, no-handed. Pablo burped loudly.

"Ever since she became a scab-faced hoor and a traitor to us girls."

"Carlotta," I said, but she snapped her long fingers in my face to shut me up.

"*Por favor,* don't make up another excuse for her. She's no good for you. She's a dabbler. She don't want no girlfriend, she want a slave, and you keep goin' back for more. You got to get some self-respect because, *chica*, nobody gives that for free."

"Yeah, yeah, I know," I said. But I was thinking there was more to it than that. Frank, for one. Vincent, for another.

"*Mira,* why you don't get a real girlfriend who's gonna like you?"

"It's not that easy, Carlotta. I'm not like you."

Nestor and Jorge rolled their eyes and pretended to barf on their plates.

131

"You think it was easy to find Pretty Boi? To get a boyfriend who treats me good? You think there's a lineup of cute, sexy boys at our school or wherever who can't wait to respect a transsexual, *Latina*, hot *mamacita*?"

Nestor snorted and said, "Well, there have been lineups for a few other things around here."

"That's right. I work my way through a million horny guys who can't get enough of me all night but don't want to hold my hand walking down the street. So, I know all about it and you got it way easier, bio-girl! So don't tell me nothing."

I was thinking how ferocious and righteous Carlotta was, how she gave me the kick in the ass I often needed. Carlotta was a real friend.

"Yeah, if Carlotta can find a half-decent boy to share lipstick with, you could get a girlfriend for sure." Nestor laughed across the table at me and even though it was supposed to be a joke I wondered if she minded. It wasn't funny to me.

"Nestor, it's all right, *Guapo*." She patted his hand. "I know you are uncomfortable with your sexuality and it make you feel like a real man to insult me, but it wasn't me calling the 1-900-Har-Dick Hotline last month every night your mama was working the late shift. We'll keep that between us. *Si*?"

Nestor turned red and stared at his plate. Jorge laughed loud, from the belly.

"Can we listen yet?" Isabelle leaned on the table and sighed. 'Lisabeth kept eating her supper like a dog, lapping up parts while still covering her ears.

"Ooh, Nestor. *Mariposa, maricon*," Jorge sang in his ear. "I'm not sharing with him no more. How can I sleep in this house if I'm the only one who's not a pervert?"

Carlotta nodded to the girls who picked their forks up right away.

"I am not," said Nestor.

"What's *maricon?*" Isabelle kept eating but was waiting for an answer.

"A faggot," said Jorge. "Who takes it up the. . . "

"A boy who likes other boys," I said. "And there's nothing wrong with that."

I turned back to Carlotta as I finished the last of my beans. "Anyways, I'm going to visit Sexy Carol tonight. I ran into her on my way over here. You should come, too."

Carlotta laughed. "You gonna have lots more to tell me tomorrow if you don't bring me tonight. May I suggest you borrow a pair of pants from one of these boys?"

I remembered what Hardcore Hank had said the other day, about moving on, and my intestines curled. I looked down at my huge boots, ripped stockings, and the bondage kilt I'd worn to the Cuntagion show. "Why pants?"

"Let me butch you up tonight," said Carlotta. "Turn you into the dream date that girl's been cryin' for."

"Carol doesn't cry for anything."

"Miss Carol been waiting her turn long enuff. We give her a chance to take it, okay?" Carlotta eyed me hawkishly, already measuring out renovations in her mind.

"You think she likes me?" I said. "What, did she say something? Come on, Carlotta! Tell me. Tell meee."

mOSH Pit

Carlotta smiled a secret, womanly smile and wouldn't say a thing. She was trying to kill me, I knew it.

Carol? I thought to myself.

Carol.

chapter eighteen:

Sexy Carol

Carol Thompson, aka Sexy Carol, worked in the east end. Far from our school and far from her grown-up beige apartment in the Annex. She didn't want anyone to confuse her academic career or her independent home life with her job. When I arrived, she was talking to some dude in a black Mercedes beside the dumpster in an alley. The tinted window was lowered and Dude's bulbous nose protruded from the air-conditioned interior.

I heard her laugh, like he was some big comedian, and her silver purse swung when she leaned her face forward, presumably to enhance her scoop neckline. She swiveled her weight onto her left high heel and brought the right foot up slightly off the ground and slowly rotated her ankle twice this way, twice that. Still smiling, she carefully shifted her weight onto the other leg and hip and slowly worked the left side. She dripped a few of her coveted blonde curls in through the window and tossed a huge handful of them away, over her shoulder, like there was just so much of it, it was such a pain to have it hanging around all the time. Meanwhile, those few swirls of manbait snaked further down the inside of the window, maybe rubbed against his face or his hand or the shoulder of his jacket.

"If even one bit of my hair touches them, they're done."

Carol told me that a long time ago, under the stairwell in the basement at school. We were skipping history. Histrionics, she called it. With a dull, wide man for a teacher who had a few long wispy hairs wound round and round to cover as much scalp as possible. Mr. Sheard. Ha ha. It really was his name. That day we smoked a joint outside at lunch and told jokes, shy dorky ones at first and grosser ones later on, the kind you usually pretend you don't really hear when someone else tells it on the bus. We joked and laughed and goofed around until it started to rain, drizzly and magic and dewy on the face.

I was staring up at the grayness when she kissed me. Soft. Curious.

Definitely not an accident.

Right along the jaw bone. She nibbled all the way over like a kitten and bit my whole chin, laughing. Then both her lips kind of grabbed onto my bottom lip and hung on for a bit and then clambered over to the top one, too. Sexy Carol kissed me with all of her worldly sophistication, all of her professional expertise, full on the mouth, while the rain poured down soaking us both. I squeezed two handfuls of that glorious hair, cradled them in my fists and kissed as well as I could right back.

When thunder started cracking open the sky we ran through the muddy yard and the parking lot, which was looking more like a reservoir every minute. Empty cigarette pack ships and rafts of potato chip bags spun crazily in the pools of dirty water. We raced inside and snuck down to the basement, still laughing, and me wondering at the suddenness of it all.

"Do you like my hair or what?" She sounded annoyed so I dropped the piece I was touching.

I looked at her carefully. She had pale, delicate eyebrows that she drew over top of with a pencil. I hadn't noticed that before. The pencil part, I mean. Her skin was smooth and perfect except for one little red blotch at the temple. Where she scratched at a blackhead, probably. She had the start of a frown line in the middle of her forehead and when I followed her slender nose along I realized she was biting her lip. Her lashes seemed huge and dark against her cheek and they left some smudges when she blinked away from me.

"I do. I do like your hair. I like to play with it. It's your trademark, I guess. But you'd look great with a shaved head, too."

"Really? You think so?" she said.

I traced my fingers lightly over her face, her high cheekbones, and tugged on her two juicy earlobes. "Yeah. You'd
look gorgeous with no hair at all."

She smiled at me then and pulled me into her and promised to shave it all off as soon as she was finished making men
her business. "No one would ever recognize me. It'd be like
starting all over, fresh, but in the same city."

And then we started over, different kinds of kissing for
that closed-in room full of heat and steam from our drying
clothes. Until the janitor arrived, that is, with a clatter of
stinking mop water and a surprised look on his face.

Obviously Carol Thompson wasn't finished making men
her business. She still had all her hair, her long shapely legs,
and enough eye makeup to distract from the intelligence in
her baby blues. She coddled Lardass, waggled a finger at
him and, still smiling, backed away from the car window.
She shook that hundred dollar hair flirtatiously, let it settle
down her back after she turned to show off her miniskirt-
ed behind.

I lit her cigarette once Mister Mercedes moved along, further east where the girls could be argued down in price a
notch. If I felt nervous around her on a regular day at school,
I was apoplectic tonight. Between Carlotta's suggestions, Sexy
Carol's outfit, and the weirdness of watching her solicit older
men for money, I was a wreck. I hid behind the bangs
Carlotta had styled for me after a shower at her place. She and
the twins had worked pomade through my hair, pulling it
down long and floppy like a giraffe's mane.

Carol was saying, "I paid more for one of these shoes than he'd pay for my whole body." She flicked her cigarette and sent miniature fireworks trailing off beside her bare leg.

"I don't get how you can be so nice to them," I stuttered. "You're so friendly, like. I'm not, even with the invisible internet guys at work."

"I'm not *nice*, I'm professional. My job is to make them feel hot and studly and likeable. I set a price and tell them what I'll do or not do. The day they realize I'm only being professional is probably the last day I'll work the skirt."

And the last day she worked the skirt would be the first day of her newly shaved head, I thought. But Carol didn't mention any hair plans. Not out loud, anyways.

"Hey, come to the Biker Boozecan with me, why don't you? Hank's band is playing tonight. Velvetine's dancing tonight too, so Diesel and some of their friends will be there."

I was getting obsessed with the idea that maybe Carol would kiss me some more, like she did that day in the rain so many months ago. Maybe this time there'd be no interruptions.

"I should make some money first." Carol's voice jumped me back to reality.

"What for?"

"I have a quota," she said. "Pay the rent, pay the bills, buy nice clothes, and match all that in my savings account. I'm gonna surprise everyone and go to med school one day. Become a gynecologist!"

When she said the last part she grabbed the fly of Nelson's baggy army pants and twisted the fabric around her fingers, pulling me after her by my miserable crotch.

"Carol!"

"What!" She laughed out loud. "Just doing some research. You don't mind donating your body to science for a few minutes, do you?" She swung me around still gripping You-Know-Where and pressed me against the brick wall, stabbing at my boots with those ice picks on her feet.

"Ha ha—stop it."

"Ha ha—no."

I close-up focused on Carol's mouth, the shape of her soft lips, pouting out the syllables large like on a big screen TV. Giant lips already memorized that I traced each night alone in my bed. Hundreds of trays of mouths, hot out of the oven part of my brain, teased me hopeful for every single one I ever nibbled. Carol finally loosened her grip on my arm and we walked together like an old married couple, slowly and in perfect step. She ruffled my flaccid 'hawk. I blushed and broke into a light sweat when she scraggled her long nails at the back of my neck. It gave me a severe case of goose bumps, among other things.

"Actually," she said, "you look like a really cute boy tonight." I sputtered and tried to cover it with a cough, and she said, "All right, Simone. Take me to the club. I could use a date with a handsome escort like you."

chapter nineteen:

So, Suddenly It Was A Date!

So Sexy Carol and I headed down to the east harbor in the warehouse district, where the rats were larger than Carlotta's baby nephew. I was freaking, since we were Suddenly On A Date. I couldn't think of a thing to say and was completely paranoid, like I was guarding the last virgin on earth from a Viagra-inflicted squadron of maniacs. Every time a car drove by, it slowed right down and unknown men leered out the windows at her. Sexy Carol couldn't have been more obvious if she were taking a second bow on stage at the Hummingbird

Centre. I always felt better on my bike around that neighbor-hood, but you couldn't very well expect a glamorous, profes-sional woman like Sexy Carol to go zooming around on a BMX, for crying out loud. She'd probably get runs in her stockings. If she had any on.

The farther we walked, the fewer people we saw. We passed the old building she used to live in, with her mother and stepfather, Uncle Creepy. Carol threw a rock at their window and screamed, "FUCK YOU!" for good measure. We kept walking and I asked was she all right and she said, "Oh, yeah. I just get really angry whenever I see that place. When I remember it, you know?" and I nodded. I knew.

Then, in a more controlled voice, she said, "I'm so glad I moved out of the 'hood."

She was the first of our gang to turn sixteen and the first to move into an apartment on her own. So, of course, we par-tied there practically every night and I crashed there quite a bit for a while. We all pitched in to clean up the place and scrammed before the Social Worker showed up on those bleary-eyed morning visits. But not anymore. Now she was a serious student and part-time sex trade worker and had early acceptance to two out of three schools she'd applied to.

Party's over.

Just about every block had boarded up buildings. Buildings with crumbling parts and glassy, lumpy front yards where people threw stuff they didn't want anymore. Mattresses and broken lamps and a smashed tricycle. Dirty diapers. Once, a long time ago, I found a book of poetry with the cover torn off it. Walt Whitman. Cherry said he was a big old fag. I said how would she know, she never even went to English class and she said, "Shut up, I just know—okay?"

Okay.

Lights flickered from the bricked bellies of those places, whispers escaped the insides like exhaust, from where people met to squat the place, or just to crash and get high. Then vanish. People shuffled around in the shadows of doorways and gathered in small macho knots, ready to explode who knew when.

Sexy Carol tried to call a cab on her cell phone but the lines were busy. "There's no way I'm walking through Little Purgatory in my new shoes."

I wasn't sure if she thought they'd get dirty or if she was worried someone might try to steal them. Maybe her feet just hurt.

"Let's keep walking and wave if one drives by," she said.

"Okay." I walked backwards, so I wouldn't miss one coming.

Then she pulled me by the belt and said, "How are we supposed to hold hands if you're facing that way," and I gulped.

I looked at her, all silver and beautiful under the streetlight, and she leaned into me and kissed me on the lips. She moved up close to me. I could feel all her perfumed girl parts pressing into me and when her kiss stopped it turned into soft talking—quiet, husky questions with her eyes looking right into mine.

"How do you like our date so far?" She kissed me again, longer this time. I kissed her back carefully. "Because I really like it. A regular non-paying date with someone cute who actually turns me on."

Turns her on!!

Sexy Carol Thompson was shining those blue lights into my eyes and then lowering those long lashes and giving me the wibbles. Sexy Carol was flirting.

Flirting with me!

If we'd been smiling any wider at each other, pieces of flesh would've cracked and split open and our faces would've crumbled to decay, just like the old houses around us.

Carol!

"Uhm." I couldn't talk while she traced my lower lip with her pretty, manicured finger. It tickled and also felt good at the same time.

"It's just I don't always know where you stand," she was saying.

Stand?

"Like if you're even single. It's hard to tell sometimes. If you're With-With Cherry or if you're Just-Friends. Know what I mean?"

My ears ached with the roar of an unbridled wind that filled my brain.

How to answer that? Where to even begin?

And then a flicker of insight danced across her brow.

"Oh," she said. "I see."

Her face. Disappointed? Was she?

The moment passed and I felt a terrible achey loss. I'd gone and ruined it all, before it could even begin.

chapter twenty:

Tom Boy Meets Aphrodite

The pervy cab driver that dropped us at the Boozecan had offered a free ride, provided we made out in the middle of the backseat so he could watch everything in the rearview mirror. Normally, I wouldn't have minded any excuse to paw Sexy Carol, but I was still floundering, reeling from the conversation that I'd botched up. Carol was pretty quiet. I wondered if she was regretting her decision to come with me. I seemed to be paralyzed by panic.

I got a wee nod from Godzilla, since I was practically a regular at the place by then. We waltzed past a small line of suburbanites, 905-ers, who were getting a hard time from security. Black Sabbath blasted us before we even got the door all the way open. Everyone looked up as we came in. Me, a Tom Boy in denim and fatigues, with Blonde Aphrodite on my arm. Leather-clad bikers stopped drinking their beer, momentarily. Carol's radiance eclipsed all the other girls. Mouths watered for her, like she was the main attraction at the Dominion deli counter or something. Her competitors paraded around, obviously trying too hard. Skinny, insecure tubes of luncheon meat in overpriced fetish wear and too much makeup.

Take that, Cherry Tart.

I hate to admit it, but I loved the look of absolute disbelief that knocked Cherry's socks right off the dance floor. I hadn't seen her in forever, had been worried sick for her, and there she was whooping it up on the dance floor. I played it up a bit, getting Carol a stool at the bar, ordering her a drink and whatnot. I was tongue-tied and jittery, desperate to make all the right moves. I stood as tall as my big boots would let me in a last-ditch attempt to Date Carol. I mean, I'd blown it but I could fix it, couldn't I? I was laying the Lady treatment on thick because I still couldn't think of a single intelligent thing to say. I made a mental note to thank Carlotta for the butch etiquette fact sheet.

Meanwhile, Cherry started dancing in earnest, competing with the paid girls on the raised platforms and in the cages, pulling off moves that might even cause deep muscle tissue damage. She ground against some guy's leg and laughed in my direction like she was having a ball, but I noticed Vincent wasn't around and she was busy twisting the old neck around to monitor Carol's and my activity. I caught myself fantasizing for a split second, that Cherry suddenly realized she was deep-down in love with me and was frothing with jealousy. But, like Carlotta, I knew it was more twisted than that. Cherry didn't want me. She just didn't want me to ever have anyone else.

"Your Special-Friend slash Girlfriend is jealous." Carol stroked the shaved parts of my head when she leaned forward to tell me this. I sensed her annoyance with the whole scene. I should've told her that Cherry might be there. I should've taken her anywhere else but here.

I said, "Carol, she's not my girlfriend. She's straight. Mostly."

"Really? Who's she with now?"

"Some dealer named Vincent. He's not here. Not yet, anyway."

"Hmm." Carol looked suspicious.

"Cherry thinks he's all that." I tried hard to sound casual.

"If it's the Vincent I think it is, I'd feel sorry for her. So when do you think you'll be getting over her? Anytime soon?"

I practically spat my beer right out. Sexy Carol stared me down and the question hung there, horribly. Then she pulled the back of my hair and licked her amazing lips right in my face. She'd obviously gotten back her sense of humor.

"When do you think you'll be ready for a real date with me?"

"Carol." I chugged some beer, then wiped my chin where it dribbled. "I don't think I'm the kind of person you think I am."

"Fill in the blank," she said. "What kind of person would that be?"

"Huh?" I tried to lower my voice. I wished I'd never brought it up. Not there, with all those virile specimens surrounding us.

I said, "Well, I'm not a player. I don't go cruising around and picking up girls all over the place. I don't have a pile of phone numbers at home, or anything."

Carol sipped her drink and listened.

"No, that's it. That's all I wanted to say."

Carol sipped some more. She was waiting. She had some nerve.

I leaned close to her and said it quietly. "I don't have a lot of experience. Not like you."

Carol opened her gorgeous mouth and poked the tiny last bit of an ice cube out with the tip of her tongue. She pushed the melting piece into my mouth and warmed my lips with another kiss. Her hair swung past me, past my face and over my shoulder and along my arm and I knew that if I was a man in a car with a lot of money, I'd want to give it all to her, too.

Just then the lighting changed and we looked up. I stepped away from her slightly and swallowed the sliver of ice that was still in my mouth. I swiveled to get a good view of Velvetine's corner. She was wearing a Wonder Woman costume and I couldn't wait to see the Magic Lasso tricks she'd been practicing on the lawn at school. Carol pulled her stool in behind me so I was standing in front, and she settled her arms around me, hands holding my belt loops right in front of my hips. I felt the heat from her thighs around me in back, too.

Her Crotch!

"Velvetine's a great dancer," she said in my ear.

148

I nodded. It was so true. I knew she sometimes had to put up with a whole lot of bullshit working here, but the actual dancing part suited her. Most nights she made a couple hundred in tips. And Diesel was sort of like her personal security system if anyone tried to get rough with her.

"God, Velvetine's got a great ass," she murmured.

I wondered if Carol meant this in a professional sort of way. Or if she was actually enjoying the ass like any guy on the premises. Any guy and me, that is. Could it be that Carol liked women as much as I did?

We watched in silence as Velvetine hog-tied some poor slob on the tiny stage. I could barely make out the back of Diesel's crew cut as she dragged guys away when they got too close to the action. Carol hugged me from behind and rubbed her face against the shaved parts of my head. Her hair made a curtain around us and it danced, satin and strange, on my bare arms.

Heaven!

I inhaled her perfume, warm and floral. Delicious. She gripped me with her knees, dug them in slightly, and I felt her breath on my neck. The hairs back there stood up and tingled. I closed my eyes. I wanted to never wake up from this dream.

"Hey, Freak!"

It was Hardcore Hank, slapping me rough on the arm and cheersing me with a bottle of Fifty.

"Don't mind me, breaking up the honeymoon over here," he said. He lurched and embraced me, almost sending Carol right off her stool.

"Hey, sorry we missed your show. Just got here."

"'At's okay," he said. "Meathead broke a couple strings so we didn't sound as good as usual. Who's the lady friend?"

Hank nearly toppled right onto us when he leaned around to get a good look at Carol. "Holy shit! Where'd you find this gorgeous babe?"

"Hank, you know Carol," I said.

Carol smiled and Hank kept it up, pretending he'd never met her before like he did every time he saw her. He took her hand and kissed it, then looked at her ravenously and started nibbling her knuckles, like usual. Then he started barking a bit and pretend swallowed her whole hand. Luckily she thought this was funny, no matter how many times he did it. Hank punched me on the arm and actually did it pretty hard so I had to rub it a bit when no one was looking. That was guy talk for "Way To Go!"

Even though Hank always acted like a real letch, he was pretty much a gentleman when you got right down to it.

"Well, if it isn't Miss Cherry Pop." Hank leaned forward to kiss Cherry's suddenly extended hand.

"Charmed, I'm sure." She kissed him on the cheek then kissed the air beside Carol's cheek. "Hi, Carol," she said. She sounded so phony. "Not working tonight?"

"No, Simone's taking me out on the town," she said.

I blushed furiously and bit my lip so I wouldn't smile too wide. Or throw up. I was hugely nervous about this scenario. The look on Cherry's face was brutal. She lit a cigarette and said, "Really." She blew smoke right into my face. "Finally got yourself a date, Simone?"

I didn't answer. She took my beer, right out of my hand, and started to drink it. She said, "Must be costing you a fortune."

Carol kissed my neck and said she'd be in the ladies room for a few minutes. "Then we can leave," she added, looking Cherry right in the eye.

She and Cherry were enacting some kind of territorial war ritual. It was way more bloodthirsty and terrifying than the male-dominated mating routines I'd witnessed my whole waking life with Cherry. Sexy Carol and her hair flitted past as she stalked over to the bathroom. Me and everyone else at the bar watched her ass and her long bare legs and those high-heeled Cinderellas. She crossed the large room like it was a Parisian catwalk.

Cherry's face had a pinched look to it. She said, "What? Half price rates 'til the chlamydia clears up?"

"Don't, Cherry." I didn't know what worried me more. That Carol was already pissed off and might leave? Or that she might stay and witness Cherry get Ugly first hand.

Cherry snapped her fingers in front of my face. "Are you listening? We got an extra shift tomorrow, okay?"

"I gotta study," I said. "Exams."

"Whateve', Simone. I gotta eat."

No kidding. She was all bone, skin stretched tight, some crazy glue holding it together.

"I need the money. You can study before and after. It's only a few hours. I'm not wrestling any of those other girls—that wasn't the deal. So meet me at eleven."

I nodded, yeah yeah, but I was distracted, trying to figure out if Carol was actually in the washroom, or if she had made her way straight out the front door.

"You'll never guess who was looking for you the other day," she was saying. Cherry moved slightly so my view to the bathroom was blocked. I didn't like the drunken smirk on her face. She tilted her chin up and chugged the rest of my beer. A challenge.

"Huh?"

Cherry sniffed loudly and rubbed her nose. "Old friend of yours. You love a man in uniform, don't you? Anyways, you missed Hank's whole set. They rocked!"

"Funny, he said they sucked. Where's your boyfriend, Cherry?"

Her face tightened and she glared at me. "Fuck you, Simone."

"No, seriously," I said. "Where's WonderDick? That's who's been holing you up all this time, right? What, is he out stealing money from some other girl?"

Cherry pushed past me. She scooped up two unattended drinks on way over to the DJ booth. She downed them both and dropped the cups on the floor behind her. I watched as she headed straight to the slimy group of guys who usually hung out with Vincent. Phony, high-pitched laughter sailed back to me in her wake.

"Hey." Carol had been standing there, off to the side, unnoticed.

I tried to ignore her face. It was too beautiful and confused right now. And also a bit angry. A scary combination for an inept goof like me. I lit a cigarette and tried to get my bearings. I got Carol another gin and tonic to stall for time. She squeezed her lime wedge and looked at me critically.

"I thought it'd be nice to say hi to Velvetine and Diesel," I said. "Before we leave, I mean." I looked up at her quickly and was surprised to see a softer expression on her face. She rubbed my shoulder and smiled at me. Diesel, with excellent timing, was heading our way, tromping across the room and parting the crowd like Moses.

"Hey, Buddy." Diesel ran her calloused hand through her crew cut, impressing all of us nearby with the muscles on her arm. She stood with her feet planted apart and cocked her head at me.

"Hey yourself, Diesel." I perked right up and grinned back at her. She looked so cool, Jimmy Dean all the way. I noticed her looking past me and lingering on Carol who was playing with the spiky bits of my hair. They said their hellos and Diesel hovered closer to Carol, flexing her strong, capable body. Diesel complimented her on the beautiful dress.

Had I?

Her perfume smelled delicious, Diesel said. I had definitely noticed it, too, but hadn't mentioned anything to Carol.

Shit!

I slipped in between them, into that shrinking and volatile space between their bodies, and patted Diesel on the back. "I loved your show the other week," I said. "When're you playing next?"

So that got her onto talking about Cuntagion, and how they were trying to set up a mini tour, and how they were maybe playing again in a month or so, but they wanted Velvetine to perform with them and she had to study for exams.

Exams!

Right on cue, Velvetine appeared in a black velvet mini-dress and her hair braided in two long lengths, wrapped in satin ribbon. She and Carol hugged each other and, although they were opposites in many respects, aesthetically they complemented one another perfectly. Diesel and I grinned, bursting with pride. They were the hottest girls in the place, and we were their dates! We were all chatting away when Diesel said I should come by when they were rehearsing sometime, and Velvetine said why didn't I bring my bass and jam with them, and Diesel said, "What? You play bass? Why dincha say so?" And I blushed and stammered and said I was only learning, that I needed to get practicing, and Diesel said, "Practice at our place, Buddy."

"We can hang, have a coupla beers, wank our instruments," she said and winked.

Winked!

And I felt just like a little kid, all goofy and excited, and I even totally forgot all about Cherry for a while. I imagined playing my bass. *Really* playing it, learning to make it sing and rip. Making plans with Diesel and Velvetine in the parking lot and watching them speed away on Diesel's motorcycle was magic. Walking partway home and holding Carol's hand and kissing goodnight and making another date for after exams and waiting to get her into a taxi was magic. Postponing our final goodbyes, walking farther together, just one more block, and then again, looping arms and shortcutting through the deserted alley, was magic. We kissed some more. It was happening. A feeling of contentment and excitement was infiltrating, was running through my veins, and filling me with a delicious pull called Hope.

And then the magic, like a tiny floating bubble, drifted up and up and popped.

chapter twenty-one:

Payback

Carol's beautiful golden hair lit up like a halo when the headlights from a quietly creeping car poured over it. She pushed my face sideways to the shadows and turned into the light, shielding me from it with her body.

"Step away from the wall, please."

I think I knew it was a cop before I even heard the voice. Something in that nervous belly of mine knew. Something inside my veins.

"Who's with you there? Both of you step out with your hands up."

Carol stood shyly, with her hands raised high, eyes wide.

"Just me and my boyfriend, officer," said Carol.

"Step out, young man."

Effen great.

I stepped forward with my hands up, thanking Christ almighty that Carlotta did her gender makeover on me tonight. I tilted my chin down and hoped for some shadows drooping along in front to look like a mustache or something manly. I noticed the front of Nestor's pants were still pulled out and twisted a bit from Carol's grip.

"Jesus, Mary, and Joseph," I said under my breath.

Carol noticed my trouser trouble at about the same time. "Sorry, Officer. We were just coming home from a party and got a bit carried away here." She draped an arm around me. "Right, sweetie?"

I coughed to clear my throat and turned a solar shade of red all at the same time. "Uh huh," I mumbled.

We heard a low laugh from behind the interrogation lights. Then the car door slammed shut.

I couldn't breathe.

Boots crunched gravel, closer and closer to us.

Exhale.

I blinked furiously into the light. When he towered in front of us, his cast shadow gave me respite and I could see. Just when I'd all but forgotten him, there stood the hulking, psychopathic pig from the Satan's Playhouse Raid.

Officer Steve.

My mouth watered and terror froze me. Carol squeezed me around the waist and with her other hand she held my dead, flopping, fish arm, the one that was tingling from leaving it up in the air for so long. She wrapped that one around her like it was some priceless shawl. She breathed into my neck but didn't let go of me, not one bit.

"We were just leaving, honest," she said.

"Not so fast," he said. He stood there an eternity, daring me to puke right in front of them both. "Not much of a boyfriend you got there."

Neither of us said a word.

"Looks more like a two-bit princess whore and a muff diving freak, in my professional opinion," he said.

And I don't know what happened next but then all of a sudden I was yelling as loud as I could and standing in between them, pushing Carol and screaming for her to run and get help and his hand was up and it cracked my skull and the screaming stayed inside my head but didn't escape the sausage fingers that clamped tight over my mouth as he dragged me into the dark, into the night. And the world opened up and the singing flames of Hell deafened me. I wanted to cover my ears but my arms didn't work anymore and anyways I wasn't inside me, I didn't live there anymore, I was up up and away, soaring high above the decrepit buildings, flapping wings of strength and beauty and truth and justice and I wasn't crouched down in the dirt, paying for my insolence and my youth, wasn't paying tribute to his evil, violent nature, his badge and perfect citizenship in the public eye. I was drifting. Far away, forever and forever.

chapter twenty-two:
Amnesia

I was slowly coming to with an overwhelming sense of loss, of grief. Failure. Something had happened. I had betrayed Carol, Cherry, my mother. Everyone I had ever known. Carol wiped my face with a damp cloth, gently. It was dark, wherever we were, except for a single candle burning on a low table.

"You okay?"

Her voice came from far away. It was difficult to understand her through the ringing, the roaring in my head. It was broken. I was.

"Simone," her lips were saying. "I'm right here."

And I was alone again, in that cold and terrible faraway place, that black hole of oblivion, and it seemed right and good that I should never come back.

Not alone and not dead. Half sitting, half slumping. Looking at shiny, black, high-heeled boots. Fishnets.

I panicked and Carol was there. Carol's perfume and Carol's pretty hair dancing on me. She held me and her small, cold fingers were telling me *I'm all right, I'll be okay, I'm a good girl.*

Bright lights stabbed me. The shiny boots clomped forward, made the floor thrum under me. I shrank farther into Carol's armpit, away from the boots.

"Jesus! A cop did that?" The shrill voice cut through my roaring head.

The stranger bent over me and her ponytail swung over her shoulder. The tip of it tickled my nose. She smelled good, like mint. Her mouth moved. There was lipstick on it. There was gum in there.

She held parts of me. Looked, touched. I didn't feel much. She listened to my quiet body rhythms, listened to Carol's broken bits of the story. I felt the vibration of Carol talking, the rumblings from her chest. I never said a word. Carol's friend looked into my eyes with a flashlight, touched the bump on my head. I jumped when she got near my ear.

"Shit," her mouth moved.

She said something quickly to Carol, they talked back and forth, then overtop of each other, and the lady started yelling, and I could hear her say, "I'm a hooker, not a doctor. Take her to the hospital!"

"Hah," I said or thought. *I hate hospitals.*

Then she yelled did I know his badge number, did I remember his face or name, and said I should press charges, that this was a serious crime and there was no doubt a lot of forensic evidence. Her eyes trailed down my body. She snapped a blanket over top of me. "Fucking cops."

I noticed I was shaking. That I couldn't seem to stop.

Carol's friend drove us to my mother's apartment, gave me some painkillers for later, and then Carol helped me up the steps and in the door and down the creaky plastic-coated hallway to my room. My mom was sleeping, barricaded in her room at the front. Carol helped me undress and got a bag of frozen peas to wrap and lay beside my face and tucked me into bed and I slept. Every half hour she woke me, asked me strange questions, her disembodied voice mixing with the endless dreams that pulled me back to night. And in the morning when I finally woke in a mess of thawed peas and wet and bloodstains, I took those little pills Carol left on the dresser. Pieces and pictures from last night were slowly floating back to me and, frankly, I prayed for the kind of amnesia those soap opera characters got, the kind that allowed you to go about your little life anew, never once looking back to all those devastating rents in the old domestic fabric. I prayed for a blameless numbing to coat my wounds.

I slept. I dreamed. And when I turned and opened my eyes, sometimes it wasn't Carol who wiped my face or felt my cheek or fluffed the pillow. Sometimes it was my mom.

Dream One: I am taking my time to go home, walking and whistling and sniffing the fragrant flowered summer night. I am remembering the touch of Carol's hair and hands and lips and I am smiling. Then . . . skip over, skip over, fast forward. Then I am lying in my squeaky, single bed. I am happy for once, curling and settling into the sheets. And I am drifting and dreaming and playing my bass with Diesel, imagining one day being in a band of my own.

Dream Two: In the dream I am wearing a blue-and-white striped sailor outfit, one my mom made me when I was really little and she was more together. I also have my red rubber boots. I am so happy. She is smiling down at me and holding my hand, walking at my little chubby-kneed kid pace and the sun is streaming from behind her making her look like a beautiful angel. And we are walking around the edge of a pond full of ducks that people are looking at and feeding. We walk all the way around the whole pond but when we get to the other side the sun is gone and it's cold and suddenly nothing seems nice anymore.

I look up to my mom's face and it's blank.

A dark shadow is all over her like a cloud and there is no recognition in her eyes. She drops my hand and stands, staring off to nowhere. I tug on her skirt and call her name. Not hers but the only one I have for her.

Mommy!

She doesn't respond and I keep crying and pulling her but she can't hear me and I think the sun took her away, that's not my mommy anymore! And finally she turns and she slowly shuffles away. Away from me and my sobbing and all that noise.

Then I woke up.

Cherry's Blog: Most Recent Entry
Friday, June 20 5:03 AM

Fate is so weird. You spend your whole night or your whole life looking for one thing. You search outwardly, you dive inwards. You scour
the evil recesses of your own soul. You go all kinds of places looking, and then you give up. You go home raging, desperate and
depressed, like it's the end. Then, there's Fate. Sitting on your front
doorstep, waiting for you. He's hot and has bleach blond dreads
and he has candy for you and a present to say "Sorry." Then you
realize that You're Sorry, too. Because if you had Faith in Fate, you
wouldn't have gotten mad and paranoid and freaked out in the first
place. You would just be the cool and mature daredevil you're supposed to be and you wouldn't scare the guy away. You should see
the most beautiful shoes he gave me! They're gorgeous shiny

patent leather stilettos with a strap around the ankle and they're Cherry Red! They match my hair . . . or they will when I re-dye it. I felt like such a slob in my crappy jeans and T-shirt, my makeup was a mess and everything, but V. made me try them on right there on the street. They're actually a bit too big and they're scuffed on the bottom a bit but V. said it's because they were the last pair at the store and some dumb bitch was modeling them during her shift, but not anymore. They're mine now. Lucky me!

Mood: Vastly Improved!
Music: PJ Harvey

chapter twenty-three:

Comatose

Hours and days ticked away in The Tomb. I didn't leave the house. Didn't want to leave the room, the bed. The less I moved, the more it hurt whenever I *did* move, the more I feared movement. It was as if The Tomb was battling with my corpse, my soul. It was colonizing me limb for limb and now threatened annexation, to move on in for good. Into my bones and blood and brain.

Carol came and went. Murmured things to my mom. Raised her voice once or twice. My mom wandered in and out of the room, distracted. Strangely put out that I was there, I thought. On about the second or third day she tentatively regrouped with a sense of purpose. To gently bathe my face, my head, my hands. To bring me soup that she reheated on the stove. In a pot. She wore an apron. She came and sat beside my bed, read a book, looked at me from time to time. The pain in my ear subsided, the roar lessened, and I was able to hear things again. My mother began to talk to me.

I listened. That's all I could do.

Later, alone. Sitting gingerly at the end of my bed. My bass leaned up against the mattress. It was dusted lemony clean.

Mom!

I stared at it. The shiny black surface reflected part of my face. A disembodied eye. A fat lip. I traced along its smoothness, left a smeary trail of finger, a smudged print.

Evidence.

It was cool to the touch.

At long last I picked it up and plucked a string. And another. I plugged it in and turned on my tiny amp.

I made a sound. It was a long, low vibration that pulled and sang in my heart. It filled my mouth, buzzed in my molars, and sent me outwards with the note, swimming in the sound and in the emotion it touched within me. I played it again and again, pressed finger pads onto the thick grooved string. It was the deep and stirring sound of infinite sadness and it poured from me like water, the rising tide within.

chapter twenty-four:

Exam

Carol arrived and forced me into a bath. She put clean clothes on the bed. Told me to dress. She threw my jean jacket at me, pulled me out of the house. When I put it on I felt the lump of Frat Guy's stolen ID, his key. I'd totally forgotten all about his crap in my front pocket, an albatross rotting since that terrible night, voodoo fouling up my jacket, my life. Carol had a fairly clean envelope that she gave me, and she waited by the nearest post office while I shuffled inside and bought stamps, copied out his dorm room address. I popped it into the letterbox, willed all that evil karma to go with it, and slammed the little metal door shut.

Carlotta, Pretty Boi, and Velvetine met us at the subway. We walked the rest of the way to school together. They talked quietly about exams, last minute study tips, and thankfully nobody said anything about what had happened. No one asked about my stiffness, the bruising around my face and neck. I wore a bandanna on my head, hair down, to cover the ugly gash above my left ear. I felt their friendship all around me, shielding me from the invasive stares of strangers, building up some kind of force field to help me heal. I just couldn't talk.

Carol said who cares about the exam. The real test, she said, was to not disappear or dry up and crumble away, dust in the wind. If I didn't even put my name on the paper she said I'd passed because I'd gotten there, hadn't I? It was as though she'd been on that same journey and now she was guiding me through it. That lonely, internal spiral. That cocooning, silent face-off with your Ambivalent Self, the completely barren core who doesn't really want to live any-more. She knew it intimately, I realized much later.

It was weird being there, at school. I'd been far enough away from that reality to notice the smell. When you're there all the time breathing it in, it's nothing. But now the gym screamed decade-old sneakers, stale B.O., warm forgotten lunches, floor polish. The ghosty echo of whistles and bounc-ing balls and squeaking shoes haunted me. Faces blurred like long-lost relatives you met as a little kid and then once more, much later, at your sperm donor's funeral. *Biological father.* All those faces from the photo album, from a life before. Strangely routine, with zero intimacy.

The cakers were there, shiny and clean, smiling and joking with each other, 'til one of them got a glimpse of my Quasimodo face and then it was all, "Shhh, ohmigod, look," with the pointing and the hush, necks craning, eyes boggling. Then they'd go back to planning their prom parties and shrieking about their dresses, where they got their shoes, what makeup they'd be wearing. Like it really mattered.

The gangbangers strutted in after the bell rang, sullen and sorry to leave the parking lot, where muscled guys slam-dunked, shot baskets, played loud hip hop. I knew two girls who danced in their crew. They nodded to me, eyes registered trauma, recovery, no words needed. How had we gotten friendly? I couldn't say. We were all rebels in our own way; sometimes that was enough. I had a theory that these days, nothing was more punk than rap. Grassroots hiphop, not blingbling-booty-corporate-Adidas crap. And what was punkrawk but the raw expression of angry, passionate, conscious people?

We were all lined up in our tiny desks, little cockpits flying nowhere. The others were gripping sharp pencils with sweaty hands and chewing nails to the quick. Frowning and scrinching up their faces and writing like mad. Teachers stood around the gym, patrolled their little areas. They were vigilant and suspicious at first, then softened after twenty minutes or so, when they all tranced out on whatever. Who knew what held their human interest outside of being our caretakers, our probation officers? I watched Ms. Flores pull the delicate chain around her neck, twist it on her finger, shift her weight to cock her hip at a jaunty angle. Right before we sat down, Carlotta had whispered that she'd seen Ms. Flores at a gay bar over the weekend.

"Tossing back the margaritas and slo-jamming with that butch. The one who works around the corner at the post office," she said and winked at me.

I knew Carlotta had been studying all weekend and hadn't been out to any bars. She was just trying to cheer me up, I guess. Carol flicked her hair, two seats ahead, and that reminded me that I should be looking at the exam. I read through the questions, skimmed pages, started back at the beginning, flustered. I twirled little bits of my hair between my fingers. I breathed. It would all be over in a couple hours, I reasoned, and then I could go back to my room.

I wanted to play my bass.

Cherry's Blog: Most Recent Entry
Monday June 25 10:44 PM

A poem for our generation:

> We run, woolly pack animals
> Abandoned by our fathers
> Betrayed by our mothers
> Raped by our uncles
> Now we storm the jailer, run wild, rabid, into the night.
> Diseased.
> We are the night.
> We bite the hand that never feeds

This is a note to all former friends, losers, and pussies. For the record, I am not "screwing up my life," like some people supposedly are saying. I am actually more alive than I've ever been. I am done with the gossip and rumors. I don't actually give a shit what anyone thinks, so whateve'. STOP calling my trashy mother's place. She's so shitfaced she can't even answer the phone. I don't live there anymore. High school is for little girls and life is for big girls. I choose life! I am making amazing money with my new "job," I have tons of new friends, I look great, and it's only getting better. I'm through with this shitbox dumpy apartment and hope the Corpse and Mommy Dearest rot in hell. Thanks for nothing, Simone, ya fucking deadbeat. See ya never. I'm out.

Mood: SOOO Over It.
Music: CRISIS "Mechanical Man"

book three:

ReveLatiOns

Cherry's Blog: Most Recent Entry
Sunday June 29 4:12 PM

Pawn City loves me and I love Pawn City. The old guy (from the commercial) is letting me use his personal computah, just so he can get a closer look at my boobies through this T-shirt. All your unwanted collectibles become cash right before your eyes. *Cha-ching!* Scam queen Cherry rides again. Everywhere I go I am the hustler, Lil' Whitey, Baby Doll, DareDevil Red. I see price tags on everything now. Mister's watch I scored at the bus stop, forty bones. Bitch secretary's designer purse, ten bones. That antique lamp I found in your living room, get me fifteen maybe, but I'd settle for five. People, too, I know their price before they even offer it up. It's tattooed on their eyelids and when they start to nod, it's all mine.

I'm supplementing my web porn with a little one on one action, thank you, Misters. They won't give me a dollar for nothing but they'll give me twenty for almost nothing. I write them love poems in the stalls of their corporate bathrooms, in the backseats of their SUVs.

Dear Suit
Your wife won't fuck you
Even your children hate you
Go home self-destruct
Love, Cherry

Simone, you suck. Traitor Bitch. Where have you been? Thanks to you I had to wrestle with some douchebag for the past four shifts. I don't have time for this crap. Stop pouting and get your ass back to work. I got us a great job, mucho dinero, for next week, so call me or else. Oh, I picked up your paycheck for you. Heh heh. *Cha-ching!*

Mood: High and Mighty!
Music: Frank Sinatra "Love and Marriage"

chapter twenty-five

Cherry Pushed Me

"You think you're the only one who likes girls?"

Cherry pinned my shoulders to the smelly gym mat and pushed her knee into my crotch. Her shiny red stiletto weapons ripped into my legs. She dragged her black, push-up bra and the two ice cream scoops of skin slowly up and down my chest, up over my still tender face and brought them back down hard, right on top of my own medium bumps.

Two more customers beeped onto our site.

"Men pay a small fortune every day to watch half-naked girls do anything. Especially get down with other girls."

"So?" I said.

"So come on, it's only one stag party. For tons of cash! God, we practically do the same thing here for ten bucks an hour! I'm tired of working so much."

"Twelve bucks. Plus we're not naked in a room full of *actual* guys who could *actually* come over and give us an *actual* hard time."

I was feeling lucky, *grateful*, that Douglas and Brian hadn't fired me. I'd left one vague message and hadn't shown up in over a week.

"Please, Simone."

I flipped her over. I pretend-choked her with one hand and spanked her with the other. More beeps went off.

"Three hundred dollars each and we can have all the drinks and coke we want. It's only for a couple hours. A hundred bucks an hour, for fuck's sake."

I said, "I don't like coke."

Cherry said, "Well, I do."

"You've been doing enough of it lately. You look like hell. Is that all you do with your loser boyfriend? You're so wired."

"Shut up," she said.

Cherry rolled away, then pushed me flat on my back and clambered on top of me.

"Easy," I said. I'd covered most of the ugly, yellowing bruises with cover-up and foundation, but it still hurt to touch.

"Vincent is really cool. And sexy. He could have asked lots of other girls, you know, with, like, experience but he picked me. Besides, he's already done lots of favors for me. I owe him. If you weren't so jealous, you'd agree."

"Since when is spending your money a favor? Did you give him your paycheck, too?"

"You sound like a goddamn guidance counselor."

"Cherry," I said. "Do you have any money left at all?"

She looked away. She didn't. Probably not even bus fare.

"Cherry, can we talk about what's going on? You're in over your head. Admit it."

"Nag, nag, nag." Cherry turned and pinned my ankles with her hands, clamped her knees and shins onto my upper body. The spike heels threatened from either side of my head. She put her bum in my face and let one rip. I'm not kidding.

"You're sooo gross!" I struggled to get away from the invisible perfumed cloud but I was super trapped. "EWWW!"

"That's for slut ho Carol and *this* one's for you!" She punctuated her sentence with another loud blast and I sputtered in disbelief from below.

"Cherry! Gawd."

She laughed and waved her bum around. "Still wanna talk about my personal finances? I got plenty to go."

"Too bad your boyfriend can't see you now," I said. "Maybe you should try that at your stupid stag party. Man, you reek!"

She somersaulted away between my legs and I scrambled back, panting.

"I know you're in trouble," I said.

"Like I give a shit."

"I saw all those credit card receipts in the garbage can. I know you're pulling some major scam for Vincent. Whatever it is, it's not worth it, Cherry." I'd seen piles of the slippery papers with different numbers and names on them, all signed in the same loopy hand: Cherry's unmistakable writing. Pay advances, cash transfers, even appliances she bought with other people's cards. Vincent took the stuff to pawn shops and the moolah went straight up their noses. Or into their pipes, since buying a rock was so cheap and it could tide you over, bit by bit, until you had enough bills to buy a proper coke bag again.

Cherry wasn't talking anymore. Just going through the motions of wrestling, face impassive as metal.

"You'll get caught," I said.

"Not if nobody tells on us, liar liar."

She got on her feet and I felt the challenge for real now. We were circling like sumo wrestlers, eyeballs glued to each other, hands out, ready to grab flesh or leotard. She was the enemy, as far as I was concerned. *She* was the traitor, who never even asked what was happening in my life, not once, not even how I got this beating. She hadn't come to see me, hadn't even called as far as I knew. Cherry didn't seem to know I wasn't the same person I used to be.

I heard another beep.

"You think you're so smart but you're not, Cherry. You're just high or strung out these days. You're leaving evidence all over the fucking place, and you don't even know it. You'll be the one to get caught, not Vincent. You're the one who signed the slips."

"Shut up," she said. She lunged and I skipped out of the way.

I said, "If he's such a big dealer how come he's always broke?"

I pulled her down, face first, to the mat and sat on her. I pushed her arm up behind her back, up between her shoulder blades and pressed hard. "How come he takes all your money? Better yet, how come you give it away?" I said this real soft, 'coz it hurt to even think about it.

"No, he never." Cherry turned her face to one side so I could hear her bullshit better. "I already told you, he needs it to front a big order so he can pay off some debts. Then these assholes will leave him alone. They're, like, accusing him of ripping them off, or something. Can you believe it?"

I flipped her onto her back to get a good look, but straddled her torso to keep her from weaseling away. She looked like a member of some weirdo Christian cult you see on Jerry Springer. Not even remotely like the girl I'd known for years.

"You're pathetic," I said.

"You don't understand because you don't even know him," she was saying. Then, "Come on, Simone. One stag party. I bet we'd have lots of fun." She said it all husky and was grinding up against me with her hips. I didn't know what else she was saying because I just turned off the volume.

Click!

Her hips insisted and I blocked out the content entirely. The stag party business, the Vincent man of the month crap. Cherry giggled underneath me, completely submissive but somehow more alive than ever. She whispered my name. I felt her breath on my cheek. Then her tongue, wet and sloppy like a dog, all up the side of my face. And it had all the erotic power of a toothpick. Cherry was perfecting the plastic, porno response that so many guys love, and it left me completely unmoved.

I had nearly let go of myself. I could certainly let go of her. I stroked her stringy hair. I looked as deeply into those bloodshot eyes as I could. I slowly reached down to her with my own lips and whispered, "No thanks."

Bam!

She slammed her knee up into my wounded crotch, hard.

"Whaddaya mean, no thanks?" she said with a sadistic smile. She flipped me and her whole demeanor changed. She kept talking, but in a totally different voice, evil Golum, harpie shrew. "All you have to do is roll around and take off your clothes. You'll get paid to fuck me, something you've been trying to do for years, you stupid dyke. We wank the groom and no one else even touches us. Three hundred dollars each!"

I forgot about the job we were doing then, the room we were in, the Web site and everything. I fought her for real, fought just to breathe, to send her suffocating weight flying, to erase the dents her body had made in mine over the years.

"What's wrong with you?" she yelled.

She shoved me back on the floor and hit at me while she ranted, and I started to cry but couldn't say a word. I was near a breaking point inside, and I didn't know what would happen if I slipped across that sturdy wall.

She was saying, "You want to be a big, boring zero like everyone else? Work the checkout at some shitty donut store? Be assistant manager some day, like your nutcase mom? Maybe one night when you realize you're shitting your whole life away in a polyester uniform you'll walk home and O.D. on your happy pills in the bathroom. Just like her."

Mommy!

"Not me," she said through her teeth. "I'm gonna be bigger than that."

Her arrows hit me right on target, shower after shower of them. She was coming down hard from another long, sleepless run, she didn't have anything left, and she was broke. Again. She was some horrible, monster version of who she used to be and I hated her. I was still pinned but I kicked and punched the air and sobbed while she slapped me, slapped my already bruised face, yelling, "We need this money, so shut up! Shut up!"

I stopped struggling but not weeping and she watched, disgusted, as though I were an insect dying slowly at the end of her pin and not at all the gallant Romeo who had loved her forever.

More guys beeped on-line.

"Why do we need it so bad? Why can't you and me get jobs like other people?"

She shook me hard and gripped my arms so they hurt.

"Not you and me, stupid. Me and Vincent." She stood up then, and towered over me. "We need that money and if you won't help us get it then somebody else will. Like your blonde ho Carol, maybe."

Not Carol.

"Bet you'd like that, eh? Bet you'd pay to watch, just like the rest of those losers."

She grabbed her cell phone from the orange crate that the TV monitor was on. She pressed speed dial. "Guys don't pay for dyke drama or nervous breakdowns, so get a hold of yourself. Okay?"

Okay.

She posed in front of the video camera, smiling and pinching her own nipples through the saggy, pink leotard while chattering away to Vincent.

It was our most popular performance yet.

I lay there, wet and snotty, shaking out ugly sounds until my throat was raw and my eyes dried right out. Then I blew my nose on the ratty tissue Cherry threw at me.

chapter twenty-six

Hey, Vincent!

"Cherry?" Our shift was over and I stood in the lobby, the video rental part, numb.

"No time to process, Simone. Vincent's picking me up." Cherry put on pink, heart-shaped sunglasses. The rhine-stones blinked at me. She stared at the two-way mirror they had at the back of the store and painted her lips fuchsia.

Brian was inside the secret office part behind the smoky mirror, no doubt cringing. He and Douglas took turns sitting in the airtight chamber, counting their money and peering out at potential porn shoplifters. Douglas was at the cash register and said, "We do have a ladies' room for your personal use," and Cherry snapped that the bathroom was too disgusting, even for her, and she would bloody well use whatever mirror she felt like. Still glaring at Douglas, she pulled a wet disposable cloth out of her knapsack and wiped around under her skirt. She dropped it in the wastebasket right beside his counter.

"If you don't like it, fix the bathroom," she said, changing her thong. She stuffed the old one in her bag and took out an aerosol can, sprayed something horrible under her T-shirt.

Douglas and I choked on the smelly invasion. It was worse than napalm. His eyes teared up and he quickly covered his mouth and nose with a yellow hankie, one he kept in his back pocket. For once, Brian must've been glad to be the witness, trapped in an airtight chamber counting money and peering out for shoplifters.

"Whoa," I said. "I think that was hairspray, not deodorant."

"Shit. You're right." She took another bottled weapon out of her knapsack and sprayed it over top of the first junk, but twice as much.

"Gawd, that's awful." I walked away, held open the door, and peered out towards the street.

Douglas' voice boomed from the back of the store and startled me. "No, you may not have another cash advance. You're way over your limit so don't ask me again." I stepped out and closed the door behind me. The sky was getting brighter even while I watched. It must've been almost six. The streetlights snapped off. I could still see a tiny star or two up there. One half of the world was safe in bed, tossing gently mid-dream, soon to shower and dress and approach the city

187

briskly, checking their watches and running for the bus. The other half, the one we knew better, was just dropping to its knees, or stumbling into familiar corners, or collapsing in a stranger's bed. Boozed up, wanked off, and tucked in for a few hours of sleep.

"We're on the cusp," I said quietly. To myself, I guess.

No one else was listening.

She pushed past me and the hem of her skirt was caught up a bit at the waistband, so I could see her entire butt from behind. She walked quickly in those secondhand, red heels, with a quirky twitch she'd never had before. Under the circumstances I could tell how much weight she'd lost. She had changed so much in only a couple of months. She leaned towards the street anxiously and hauled on her cigarette. The thought hit me before I could stop it and I felt badly. Ashamed, in a way. That after everything, she was the girl who had banished my miserable loneliness with her outrageous glamor. And now she looked like a cheap, skiddy hoor, desperate for a fix.

"Cherry, for godsakes, your skirt."

I guess right about then tires screeched and a car peeled up. The front tire bumped up and over the curb, and the engine shook the whole frame. It barely missed us standing on the sidewalk. Sure enough, it was his junky, rusted Honda Civic.

"Hey, Vincent!"

Cherry looked through the cracked windshield at him with something dangerously close to devotion. She was a lost cause. Her whole body strained forward and, without a word

188

to me, she flew to the passenger side, wrenched the dented door open, and slid over to Vincent.

With the door wide open, I could see inside and it was full of crap. Lucette popped her head out and waved hello with her drippy tongue. She jumped onto the sidewalk and trotted over to me. I was petting her and cooing stuff and realizing I hadn't seen her (or Vincent) in a while, and noticing her nose was dry and she seemed taller and longer and skinnier than the last time I'd seen her. She'd done some growing. She snuffled my ear when I crouched down to hug her. *Whiskerytickle.* I'd been missing her and our games and the running around alive feeling in the middle of this urban cemetery. While all this was registering in my brain, Vincent whistled sharply, yelled, and swore until Lucette whined and finally climbed back into the car. The door slammed shut.

The engine revved, the muffler backfired, and the tires squealed. An early bird Suit, a nine to fiver, honked when they bounced off the curve and cut him off. The car swerved erratically into the other lane and then it peeled around a corner and that was it.

They were gone.

Cherry's Blog: Most Recent Update
Saturday July 5 11:07 PM

Dear Simone/Roxy,

Right now you're sitting on that stinking mat all by yourself wondering where I am. Just like I did for how many shifts? Sucks, doesn't it? I have a better job at the moment that pays a fuckwad of money. Hope you have to wrestle with that hairy bitch Angela. She sweats a lot. Love, Cherry.

Mood: Righteous
Music: Lesbians On Ecstasy "Tell me does she love the bass"

chapter twenty-seven:
Lazy Afternoon

Sexy Carol was talking but I had a hard time listening. She's so beautiful, my ears simply couldn't function at the same time as my eyes. We were on her balcony porch shaded from the sun and there was a nice breeze blowing around us. It sent whiffs of her flowery perfume up my nose, right into my brain. It teased her blonde curls and sometimes she had to push those stray baby bits out of her face and tuck them behind her ears, and I could hardly stop myself from reaching out to grab handfuls of the golden stuff. My skin shivered with a sudden body memory from that other night, her hair cascading around and the subtle weight of its landing, its silky trails on my face and neck and then lower.

Carol propped her gorgeous legs up on the porch railing and unwrapped the popsicle I brought her. She was wearing faded cutoffs and a little tank top. Her sexy feet were bare except for little silver rings shining on her toes. I felt shy around her again, even though we'd seen a lot of each other, what with all her rescue home visits.

She waved her popsicle at me. "You don't have to thank me, Simone."

"I want to," I said. "For staying with me and looking after me. For visiting. Everything, really."

Kickstarting my mother towards reality. Saving my life. You know.

I was feeling quite a bit better, so naturally I'd relapsed into panicked shyness around her. I grinned moronically. I tugged at the back of my Mohawk. Nervous tick. I rammed my popsicle in my mouth. It was cold and dry and my lip stuck to it so, when I let go, the blue thing hung there stupidly, pulling at my frozen skin. Carol's eyes widened. I gave it a yank! and off it came, pulling some delicate lip skin with it. Horrified, I picked the tiny piece off the popsicle and carefully daubed at the tingly raw lip part with my tongue tip.

Shit!

Carol was saying something about finals, some exam we had or something, and all I could think about was what would I say when she stopped talking. My lip stung. Carol was telling a story. She laughed and her lips and tongue were stained a faint blue. I had no idea what she was on about. I was having trouble breathing and my shoulders were tense. My popsicle dripped.

"Hey." Carol touched me and I flinched. "So when are you asking me out on a real date? We're done exams, you know."

Where was Carlotta when you needed her, with all her finesse and romantic advice!

I took a deep breath and spoke slowly, in control. "Uh, I haven't figured out what we should do yet."

Carol said, "You could start with picking a day. Not weekends, I usually work then." And she waited like a millisecond or something and then she said, "Unless you don't want to, Simone. Am I being too pushy?"

And I was, like, freaking out, thinking ohmygod I soo want to date you but at the same time I was like totally shocked that she didn't already know this, that she didn't seem to know that anybody on the planet would give their left nut just to be with her. While all this rapid-fire panic stuff was happening in my head, she was leaning farther away in her chair and that beautiful face was closing up shop, eyes looking down, chin tilting to the right, away from me.

Shitshitshitshit!

"Is it because of Cherry?" she asked quietly. "Are you still in love with her?"

I said, "Fuck no, Carol. Geez. I'm not in love with Cherry. To be honest, I don't even like her. I don't even talk to her, now." We wrestled together a few times a week, if she showed up for the shifts, but we rarely made conversation. We just fought.

Ugly flashbacks of Cherry and Vincent getting high, horrible memories of her face contorted with rage and power, her lip blistered from the homemade crack pipe, her hollow laugh ripping through me like an automatic weapon—all made me shudder.

"I think I hate her," I said. "I'm worried and angry and so sad about her." My voice cracked and suddenly I was about to cry. In front of Carol Thompson. This could not be.

After a bit she said, "I didn't know how much this was tearing you up. Maybe it's too much right now. What with everything," her voice trailed off and we both knew what she meant by that. "I'll back off. Okay?"

"Please don't," I whispered.

Then she said, "It's just . . . I think there are things that you want and you should let yourself have them. I don't believe Cherry ever intended to give them to you. Not really."

Damn that Carol.

She was right. There were things I wanted. Was addicted to wanting. Cravings like sugar. Candy kisses. Water.

"I wish you'd let someone else give it a shot," she said. "Like me."

I gulped. I couldn't even look at her. I squeezed away a couple salty drops and sniffed a bit. Carol looked at me like she could see all the way through. Like she'd been practicing looking into me for a long time and now she had it down pat. My foot was doing a nervous little jiggle all on its own. Tapping out an S.O.S.

"So," I said, wiping my nose on the back of my hand. "You're like this sex philosopher? You could have your own talk show, you know, analyzing people and doing therapy live with a studio audience."

She said, "Listen, I'm practically a psychiatrist in this line of work. You're dripping."

I blushed.

"Your popsicle, I mean." Carol laughed and I saw the blue flesh of her tongue. I blushed even more.

She sucked the end of her popsicle. She shook her hair away from her face. Blue ice melted and ran down the length of her stick then dripped onto her white top. "Shit, it's ruined." When she rubbed at the stain she ended up shaking more drips down her front. They splattered onto her crotch and thighs.

Seeing Carol flustered made me feel more confident, somehow. I sat up taller. "Don't worry," I said. "I'm really good at doing laundry! Make as big a mess as you want." I laughed and attacked her with my popsicle, too, and she smiled at me wide, then deep throated both of them together.

I wanted to, so I did it. Before I could freak out, I sucked the bottom part of my popsicle and moved down its frozen length and got closer to her mouth. I pulled mine out first by the little stick and then hers. I bit off the tip and slowly, gently, offered it to Carol's mouth. Like how she did with the ice cube, so long ago at the club.

I didn't move. I closed my eyes for anonymity. The ice was freezing my tongue, especially around my piercing. It was melting and pooling up in my mouth and any second it was going to slobber right out and all over us both. I opened my eyes and saw her smiling at me.

She moved in and took what was left between my lips and she didn't back away. The ice melted between us, in both our mouths, and we moved slow, magic. Cold parts and warm parts and it was the most delicious stickiness in the history of kissing.

Carol straddled me on my chair and her huge heavy hair made a curtain around us when she leaned her forehead against mine. I rubbed the blue circles on her top with a soft, curious finger.

"Guess maybe you should take this off and let it soak." I grinned at her.

The Tide commercial that never was.

"What do you know about it?" Carol licked my lips. She leaned back, pressed into my bladder, and lifted the top up and over her head. Her hair poured through the neck opening for hours, it seemed. The blonde curls fell against her bare back and I couldn't tell which was softer, her skin or that fucking hair. Just the way I remembered it. Carol threw her tank top backwards over the porch balcony to the sidewalk and lawn below. To be discovered by one of her peevish neighbors, no doubt. Some avid gardener.

We dropped the goopy sticks in their own blue puddles on the floor.

Topless, she pulled me by the hand into the sun-soaked bedroom. I settled in her crumpled sheets. My heart thudded in my throat. She tugged at my shirt. Cherry's shirt. Some cut-up, cotton sports thing meant for a ten-year-old boy. I traced the felt number on my shirt and bit my lip. Maybe she knew I was afraid. She turned away and I snaked outta the thing and slithered under the sheets. Then she slowly, deliberately, pulled my cotton shield away.

She touched me and I realized in all my handful of actual physical encounters with girls, and all my millions of fantasies of them, I never got touched. I did all the touching. I tried to move away, to reach out for her but she stayed my hand, said, "Shhhh," kneeled above me. I kept cringing, terrified. She touched my collarbone, light as a feather. Shoulders. I never had them until that moment. Her shimmery, fairy kisses dropped around on my skin and those small fingers fluttered around, noticing all kinds of parts I never thought about. Not on me, at least.

Earlobes. Voice box. Eyebrow. Rib cage.

Then I felt less dead. Less petrified. And I touched her back. Not the way I always imagined I would, but like she was touching me. I wanted to, but didn't touch her breasts. Even though when she moved around, they came right near my face and they were perfect and maybe I touched around the edges to make the nipples stand up but that was it, and she wouldn't touch mine either and it was killing me. She let hers tease me. I felt them pressed along my back and I sighed. And it seemed like forever when she finally rolled me over and she slowly climbed on top of me and lowered herself down so ours matched up and she let me feel them that way, over top of me and she breathed in my ear a little noise when I did it and our legs stretched out long together and our feet rubbed toes and other foot parts and the lava hot press of her crotch was right above mine.

"Why me?" I said. "I want to know."

She whispered, "Because I've always liked you." She kept kissing and licking the same spot on my arm. The soft underside part that never existed before.

She said, "I can't be your girlfriend. You know that. Right?"

I nodded. But something tightened in my throat and I wanted to say *Why not? Why the fuck not, Carol Thompson? I would be such a good girlfriend! I would be your best girl-friend ever!*

She held my face and kissed me and I tried to forget about girlfriends or not girlfriends, and I held her head, too, with that hair all around us again, and we meant it. Like in the movies. Only better.

Carol said, "I can be different with you."

"Who are you being?" I leaned over and we were facing each other on our sides and no one was on the top and no one was on the bottom. Her eyes drank everything in.

"Me," she said. "I think."

And this is how we spent the whole sticky, lazy afternoon.

chapter twenty-eight:

Score!

"No way."

"Way. I'm totally serious!"

I gave Carlotta the Look so she knew I wasn't lying. She smiled wide at me, slapped my arm, called me *chica*.

"You fucked Carol Thompson?!" Pretty Boi's mouth hung open. He delicately covered it with a swishing wrist movement and held the pose. Then he high-fived me, hugged, and gangbanger saluted.

"Stud," said Carlotta.

I blushed. "Come on, now."

"Super Stud," said Pretty Boi.

I couldn't hold back any longer so I grinned and shuffled my feet and said, "Yeah, guess I scored."

"Finally," said Carlotta. "*Dios mio*, we thought you were never gonna get it."

"So?" said Pretty Boi. "How'd it go? What's the status? One nighter? Are you Going Steady?!" He jumped up and down and clapped his hands.

"Easy now," I said. "You don't want to marry me off right away, do you?"

Carlotta and Pretty Boi studied me from a distance. They looked so proud. Like Parents.

"Did you try that move, the light her cigarette but look deep in the eyes the whole time and don't set her hair on fire move?" Carlotta mimed it smooth as silk and added a few mambo steps.

"Naw. Just tried to relax, you know. Tried to not make a fool of myself, but . . ."

"But she's a fool for love!" sang Pretty Boi.

I laughed. "Yeah, I s'pose. I just may be."

"Score!"

Cherry's Blog: Most Recent Update
Tuesday, July 22 2:12 AM

Bonnie and Clyde equals homicide.
Me and V. Smith and Wesson.
Six rounds ain't enough.

> **Mood:** Invincible
> **Music:** Fucknuckles "Quest For Cock"

chapter twenty-nine

Dime Store

"We're talking about Cherry," I said. "Not some dime-store crack whore."

"Well, I'm telling you what I saw," said Hank. "Don't shoot the messenjah. You don't believe me, you can ask Pete, Meathead, Tara Ding Dong. . . who else was there. . ."

"Which Pete?" I said. Like it mattered.

"Pete Mosqueet. French Pete. You know." Hank tossed his butt into the street and produced another beer from inside his leather jacket.

"Thanks, man." I drank while we walked away from Satan's Playhouse and the end of night chaos. The bars had all let out and it was pandemonium. People were yelling and screwing around, drunk, eating pizza slices you got at the corner. I watched a girl sitting on a stoop lean forward suddenly and vomit into the gutter.

"So what are you saying, Hank? First you give me the big 'Time To Move On' talk, and now what? You're saying I should get involved? What about the whole lemming thing?"

"Well, I'm saying, it's like, situation's way worse than we thought. So we should try and do something about it." Hank hiccuped at me, eyebrow arched.

"Like what, Einstein?" I guess I was being selfish, but I just didn't think I had it in me. I hadn't been out at night in a long time. Since the night the thing happened. I hadn't seen Hank in forever. Things in my life were finally working loose, like a baby tooth you outgrew bit by bit. Why fuck it all up now?

"You know Pete Mosqueet's cousin SkankTank? You wouldn't believe the shit he's saying about Cherry. I pounded the fuck outta him but now I'm hearing from a couple other sources that maybe the story's for real."

My stomach tensed.

"Fuckin' hope not, 'coz no way am I apologizing to that sonuvabitch. Not a fuckin' chance," said Hank. He drained his beer and chucked the bottle into the street. We both flickered a smile when it smashed into a billion glittery diamonds.

"Back to the story, Hank!"

"Well, Skank's been into the PCP for a long time, right, and he hangs with a buncha goofs from Thunder Bay or some bullshit. Well, Pete thinks maybe he's been getting into the crank lately. Hangin with some ugly mofos, got the crackwalk goin on, his old lady gave him the boot, and he's out there stealing toaster ovens and crap, trying to sell for a few crumbs, right?"

Hank stopped to light a smoke. Hank was having trouble walking, let alone telling the story.

"And. . .?!" I was impatient.

"Listen, wouldja? Ah, fuck. . . my laces!"

Hank tried to fix his boots by balancing on the right foot and bringing lefty up to retie the laces. Every time he brought his left foot up and got busy on it, he leaned and swayed over, and ended up face in the pavement.

"Have a seat, why doncha?" I said.

Hardcore Hank sprawled on the sidewalk with a bent cigarette hanging out of his mouth. He tried once more to get the shoelace thing under control.

"Need some help?" I said. I was feeling bad about being pissy with him. He's a good guy after all, and never did anything to hurt me.

Except sleep with Cherry.

Hank threw the broken cigarette into the gutter and stretched out his legs. He seemed to have forgotten all about the boot fiasco.

"Red." He looked at me grimly.

"What?"

"Red. That's what SkankTank kept calling the girl he's doing the B&Es with. Some skinny fucker with the blond dreads hooks him up, he and the girl—Red—do the deed, they meet up at the pawn shops and even up."

I didn't tell Hank I already knew Cherry'd been pulling that stunt for a while. That anyone who logged on to Cherry's live diary could find that out. Hank didn't own a computer and refused to acknowledge these recent waves of technology.

Hank said, "Problem is, SkankTank's got the biggest mouth this side of the Bloor viaduct, says they started into some holdups. Going for the cash."

"Hank, what are you on about?"

A car full of Piss Drunk Cakers flew by with some lame-ass music playing, blonde girls tossing their salon hair around in the back of Daddy's car.

"I'm trying to tell you what that broad's been up to. Heisting liquor and grocery stores with her Fuckwad Boyfriend and Skank. That pencil dick Skank's been mouthing off all over town that they been hitting up stores, cranking a load, and throwing their money around. It's a fucking disaster. Cops are looking for them all over the place 'cause they shot some guy at one of the checkouts, but only in the foot."

Only!

I sank down to the concrete beside Hank. I couldn't talk. This was way worse than I imagined, too.

"Simone?" Hank tapped my boots with his lighter. "Hey. Guess I shouldn't have told you all that, eh? I was right fuckin' pissed when I heard it. Like I said, I punched the guy's lights out. Straight up Molly wopped him, for real."

"Do you think it's true, Hank?"

He didn't say anything. I nudged him to make sure he was still awake. Conscious.

"Do you?"

I thought back to the last time I actually saw Cherry. It was in the lobby at work. She looked like total crap. Dark bags under her eyes, greasy hair, dirty track pants on. Her voice was high and rushed and speedy, and she kept looking over her shoulder, twitching around and asking Brian for money. Douglas threw her out, threatened to call the cops and everything. Told her not to come back, unless she got cleaned up and paid back what she owed them. She left, screaming obscenities at them the whole way, and only let go of me, out on the sidewalk, when I gave her twenty bucks.

"Well, Simone. I do. Truth is, like I said, I saw her a few days ago. She was a right royal mess. Total Dime-Store. I shit you not."

I sat, and the words weighed on me. I felt clarity taking root. I became sober. My anger ate up that bleakness, the quiet despair that had been hunting me, and all that dallying fear was gone in a moment. I made a decision. I was seeing things differently these days. I wasn't the same person I used to be, I reminded myself.

Hank was still yakking on and trying to light his crappy smoke, saying, "Fuck, I'm sorry, Simone, I guess I just never know when to quit jabberin.'"

chapter thirty:

No Show

"Well, this is real lame."

"Yeah. Lame-O."

Me and Diesel stood around the bar at the After Hours. We sipped at our beers and kept scanning the crowd for any sign of Cherry or her demonic boyfriend. I was still high from the joint we smoked and also from riding here on the back of Diesel's motorcycle.

1994 custom Fat Boy.

It was hard to focus on anything but the tightness in my thighs from stretching wide across the seat and the remembered crush of my chest on the back of

Diesel's leather jacket. Not to mention the vibrating engine.

Holy.

"You sure she's coming?" Diesel checked her watch again and shook her head. "I don't know, Buddy."

"Not really. I mean, I just assumed. I haven't seen her in a while, mind."

Diesel said, "I'll ask around. Hang tight, Buddy," and sauntered away, said her hellos to all the big old guys, cheersed a couple folks, worked her way around the place. Diesel knew pretty much everyone, so if there was news on Cherry she'd get it.

Biggest star on the movie screen, Jimmy Dean.

Twenty minutes later, Diesel was back. She tapped a smoke on her pack, then lit it with a flourish. Snapped her Zippo shut.

"Well," she said, with the cigarette clenched in her teeth, "She hasn't been in, not the last few nights. Dunno. Her boyfriend's in some big trouble. Owes the wrong folks a lot of money, so he won't be coming round here."

I nodded.

"If she so much as shows her face I told them to sit on her and give me a call."

"Thanks, Diesel."

"No probs, Buddy. Time for Plan B."

I probably would've said something but my mouth was dry and pasty. I swallowed more beer and thought about that dude Hardcore Hank was talking about. Him and those other guys she'd been partying with, those sketchpad friends of Vincent. I knew they'd be the ones to tell me where she was.

"Maybe you gotta let this one go, Buddy. Any girl that's hiding so hard is probably in no condition to be found," said Diesel. "I suggest you give that other girl a call. Sexy Carol!" She spun me a quarter, round and bright.

I smiled at Diesel and she roughed my hair up a bit, called me Slugger, even though I'd already explained about Carol not wanting a girlfriend. Even though we both knew she'd be working. I knew Diesel didn't want me running around after Cherry, but I also knew she wouldn't leave me hanging, either. Outside in the parking lot, Diesel leaned on her bike and smoked while I came up with my next plan. The red tip of her cigarette glowed in the night and I watched as she checked the pager clipped to her belt. She exhaled smoke and her eyes followed its trail, wispy and slow, curling up in the hot night towards the glittering stars.

That pull in my thighs mixed with the pull in my groin and the sweet pain of both carried me the last of the way across the asphalt. The quarter shone in my hand.

"Sure you're okay out here?"

I nodded. I'd decided to follow a tip from one of Vincent's fucked up friends. One more pilgrimage for Cherry, in memory of our friendship. *Rest In Peace.* I had to make the effort and I had to do it alone. End of story.

So Diesel dropped me in the east end, on the corner of Derelict and Destitute, and peeled off into the night. Back across the city to Velvetine and their very own mysterious Lesbian apartment.

Ever since Velvetine ran away from home and moved in with Diesel, the rest of us had wondered what the setup was like. An older, butch girlfriend with a job and everything. They kept meaning to have us over but never got around to it. That's what Diesel said, so nobody felt bad about it or anything. Just curious. Anyways, I was pretty sure I knew what they *didn't* have. No drunk mothers and their raping boyfriends. No social workers showing up at the crack of nine, Monday mornings. Not a squat. Not a park. Not Hank's house. Actually, I had no clue what it would be like.

Before she took off I asked her, "Hey Diesel, whatcha doin' tonight?"

She said, "I'm gonna get home, grab a beer, turn on the TV, and watch some crappy show until Velvetine gets so annoyed she takes her clothes off bit by bit and throws the little scraps around and all she has left is a flimsy sequined g-string which she'll probably stuff in my mouth. Then we'll . . ."

"Oh," I said quickly. My face burned bright. "I get it."

"Well, after all that business," she grinned and punched me a bit here, "after all that caterwauling and whatnot, we'll dress up pretty, hightail it over to our favorite dyke bar and have us a couple drinks. And that's when you'll pop up and have a couple drinks, too, and tell us all about this secret mission you're on now. Kapeesh?"

And off she sped. Into the night.

I was unnerved without Diesel and her loud motorcycle. No Sexy Carol on my arm. No girl posse. I felt ghosty eyes on me, hidden in the shadows, as I made my way alone. I knew in my bones that I had no choice. That fucking pig had done much worse than bend me to breaking. In one night, he had stolen a part of me that I almost couldn't name. More than confidence. It was that quintessential part of me, that intrinsic survival element. The part that allowed me to skate along freely, to know myself, and to know how I could handle myself in different situations. I needed to get that back and somehow it was all twisted up with seeing things through with Cherry. In my mind it had become a rite of passage, unavoidable as sin.

chapter thirty-one:

Cassandra

"Cassandra, right?" I seriously thought I had the wrong woman but she turned and gave me the eye. "You know Vincent, right?"

She rocked back and forth on the heels of those half-broken pumps. She mumbled something. She wiped her snotty nose with her hand. She lurched closer to me, eyes wide and staring, greasy hair tufted up like a wild woman.

Sergeant Major Bed Head.

Some guy walked by and she lunged over to him and grabbed his arm.

"Gimmee two dollar. Pleasepleasepleaseplease."

He shook her hand loose and kept walking down the sidewalk.

"Asshole!" she yelled. She went back to rocking on her toes and swinging her arms back and forth.

"Where's Vincent? Someone told me I'd find him here."

Cassandra used to hang with Vincent, maybe one or two summers ago. We'd be on our way home to bed and see her just on her way out for the night, out in her silver shortshorts. Before that, when she was like fifteen or something, she was a model. She lived in Europe and had photos in magazines, worked the runway. We'd see her on Fashion TV. *Local Girl Makes Good!* All the girls wanted what she had. Then . . . I don't know . . . the rumors started up, her career ended abruptly, and she came back here. She'd be at all the parties, posed on the flyers and invites. Then she was hanging outside the clubs more than inside on the dance floor, and then she wasn't hanging anywhere at all. To be honest, I'd forgotten all about her until tonight.

"Where is he?!" I surprised myself by yelling, by feeling hostile.

"Burn the red witch," she hissed, her eye fixed on mine. She looked away.

I considered making a run for it. Just dropping the whole Rescue Mission and hightailing it out of the east end, right over to the Nice Lesbian Bar to wait for Diesel and Velvetine. I could order a drink with my fake ID if the regular bouncer was back from her vacation, or try and talk my way in with the new Terminator Fascist who turfed me last time. Far away from this cracked out graveyard with crumbling buildings for tombstones and ghouly ghosts like Cassandra, drifting through scrub grass in the empty lot, haunting the place.

"You know the guy with the long blond dreads?" I said.

"I know what he look like." She stopped shuffling around and looked right at me. She didn't even sound crazy now. It shut me right up.

"He's with a girl. A redhead," I said. "Did they go in there? Please."

"Give me money," she said. "First you give me money."

"All right. Only if you tell me where they went."

"How much?" She started to get all excited again. She stepped closer and I could see her bad skin and the looseness of her teeth. "I want two dollars. No, I want five dollars! Yesss . . . I want five dollars."

She clutched my sleeve and I almost retched. I panicked for a moment, consumed by the idea that her skin and teeth and hair and her horrible, horrible stench was contagious, that those broken dirty nails would stain my shirt and the stain might travel, evil, infectious, up through the skin of my arms and rot me from the inside out, just as it was doing to her.

I wanted to smack some sense into her jittery, twitchy, Crackhead Self. Ready to betray the nation for a lousy five bucks, when she used to be so beautiful and tough and strong.

"I'll give you three," I said.

A calculating meanness flashed from her eyes but she grabbed the coins when I shook them out in my hand.

"There," she said, pointing down a darkened alley that ran alongside the boarded up building nearest us. "King Vincent go down there with the red witch."

Bring me back her head.

I was starting to hate myself for how I'd treated her, so I slipped her another two bucks. Penance.

She said, "I used to be pretty, too, you know," and disappeared into the shadows.

I heard a rustling of leaves and a snapping of twigs, then all was quiet. Just the sounds of the city. Cars in the distance rolled past like waves, and farther away there were sirens, and every now and then I heard a voice raised up like an offering in the night.

chapter thirty-two

Labyrinth

A narrow, worn path led around the side of the old building. I was freaking, half expecting someone to rise up from any bush and pound me into oblivion again. My blood was still tainted from that recent soul-killing defeat. I breathed loud, hot, to steady my nerves. I walked quietly to the back door and found it open. So I went in.

The smell knocked me back. My eyes adjusted to the dark. It was a long hallway, doors on either side. Some were closed, two-by-fours nailed over top. Some had no doors at all and some were being pushed open by the zombies going in and out. I felt the warm press of the knife in my hand, deep in my pants pocket. I imagined Cherry, wondered if she was as scared as me right then.

Not much happening in the first room. A few people crashed out. Nodding off. Broken furniture, couple of sleeping bags. Some guy passed out on a dirty table with his works still half stuck in.

No Cherry.

Next door was the remains of a washroom. The toilet seat was gone. Brown smears on the wall and it looked like sprays of blood up there, too. The charred remains of a soap dispenser hung on the wall above where the sink used to be. It was smashed on the concrete floor and covered in fluids. A small movement from the far corner caused a new panic. *Rats!*

I ran down the hallway, choked back the bile that burned the back of my throat and breathed, nice and deep. I was trancing out again. Like in the alley, floating and watching from high above. Slightly surprised by every move you see yourself make and completely unable to intervene, no matter how passionate you may feel about the situation. I kept walking, looked in most of the doorways. I saw things that I didn't always understand right away. Movements, bodies leaning together in jerky stuttered motion. Loud voices, screechy and rough. A crusty old guy beetled out of one room and zipped into another. He didn't even see me, only his empty coke can that he shook and the rock he was about to fire up. I peeked in the room where he scored and sure enough there was some action. Not Vincent. Some other dealer and his crew, and I didn't see Cherry, so I backed out without getting their attention and hardly breathed while I watched myself shrink away.

Parts of the banister had been ripped out of the wide staircase and a couple of the steps were caved in.

Turn around! Get out of here!

But no, I walked up calmly. My head pounded with the urgent warnings of the Floating Watchful Me, but I walked on and up and just missed falling through on a weak spot. And at the top I saw a large room with double doors, and most of the glass panes were broken. Some dude and a girl were collapsed in a love seat setting up their works. I'd seen people mainline before, but not right up in my face like that. I watched her tie off, and sit, preening, waiting for it like an alley cat as he banged it into her, quick. Her face relaxed, eyes closed, then the smile broke over it, wide. He had trouble doing himself, finding a vein I guess, and ended up skin popping with the same needle, jabbed it in and it wasn't the first time 'coz there were all these deep bruises along his arm, lying wait under the skin like a cancer, ready to bloom and grow. Later I saw that same girl somewhere else, dancing, even though no one else was. No music, either.

Cherry wasn't there. Not anywhere.

chapter thirty-three

Velvetine and Diesel

Velvetine and Diesel would make a gorgeous postcard.

All four of them.

I tried to not watch them too much while I smoked on the stoop, ducking back out of the rain. They leaned blurry against the streetlight and kissed. They didn't care about getting wet. Rain ran all down Velvetine's long, black hair, all over her faces and both blurry Diesels held that tiny waist and also held the back of those girlie heads, gentle like.

I shook my head and stared hard until they sharpened into focus and there were only two of them. Diesel kissed and kissed her, and Velvetine did this crazy thing girls do. She twirled her hand at the back of Diesel's neck, tickled those short stubbly hairs at the back of her crew cut. They smiled while they kissed and whispered stuff to each other, and I really wished I wasn't there.

I dreamed up Carol, tasted her name for a moment. I wanted what I saw so badly I could feel that lonely ache. Someone to twirl my hair. Someone's hair to twirl.

I tossed my butt into a puddle and lurched off into the night.

About three blocks later I heard yelling and running and it was Diesel, out of breath right up behind me. She grabbed my shoulder and shook the water off her face.

"Holy, you walk fast. Where ya going?" She coughed and wheezed a bit but kept her big paw on me. "I gotta quit smoking. Those things are killing me."

"Oh, I just didn't want to be in the way, is all. Don't worry about me, I'll be fine. I'll catch you later, okay?" I pulled away but her iron grip didn't let up.

"No way, man. Listen, I'm sorry. I'm pretty drunk and I'm rude at the best of times. Wasn't thinking, is all. I got plenty of time to make out with Velvet. You can't blame me for being smitten, is all. She's my kryptonite."

I backed away.

"Come on. We want you to stay over." Diesel wiped some rain out of her eye and smiled. "This is no night to sleep in the park, hey."

"I could go home," I said. And I realized it was true. I had a key. It was there, waiting. Way more than lots of people had, that's for sure.

"Yeah, Buddy, but it's pouring. Your mom's place is so far away. Come on."

I was thinking *Please don't be nice to me right now, please just leave me alone.*

Diesel tugged my arm. "Buddy, you're soaked!" I exhaled and Diesel pulled me into a hard, wet hug. "Besides," she said, "Velvetine'll kick my ass if I go home without you."

I did a small laugh into Diesel's shoulder but before I knew it I wasn't laughing, I was actually shaking and crying, but Diesel thought I was having a chuckle so she slapped me on the back, and that's when I gasped and really let it out and cried away on that great big, black, leather lapel like nobody's business. I cried until I puked up all that alcohol over the outside of a slippery wet postal box, clung to it like a Pavlovian monkey to its re-assigned, metallic mother. And all along Diesel put that strong arm around my shoulders and talked softly in my ear like I was a startled horse or something, and rocked me back and forth gently. Her huge hands massaged the back of my neck and patted my shoulder blades and ruffled up my dripping mop of hair. I cringed at first but there was no escaping them and suddenly I realized it was such a relief. I couldn't remember the last time anybody touched me. Carol? I shivered and hung limp around her neck while Diesel swung me like some overgrown baby, saying, "Shh, shh. Hey, it's okay. Let it go, Buddy. Let it go."

Then I rinsed my mouth with rainwater until the horrible taste faded.

Diesel walked me along a bit and said did I want to talk about anything, like maybe did I want to talk about the whole Cherry thing, or any other thing? Like, maybe what happened to me? Like about the pig who hurt me? And, had I noticed I wasn't quite the same? Or maybe did I want to talk about whatever my Secret Mission was earlier that night?

And I said, *No.* "No way, man, but thanks and if I ever get the words together I know where to go," that sort of thing.

Then she said something about how alcohol brings out hidden emotions sometimes, and it just meant I had to get in touch with my damaged emotional self . . . no, my stunted emotional growth . . . or something. Then she slapped me on the back again and kept her arm around me, and said, "Simone, you remind me of me when I was like fourteen. Or twelve. Didja know that?"

And I said, "No."

And she said, "You're like my queer little brother, or something."

And I said, "I'm a girl, Diesel, I'm a fucking girl."

And she said, "Buddy, I know what you are, so simmer down. You can be whatever you want, I'm just saying you remind me of when I was a teeny bopper. Mind, I matured early, like a million years ago. Hahaaahaha." Diesel was walking me faster and faster this whole time, until we were trotting along through the puddles. She laughed and stomped tidal waves of dirty street water all up my army pants, right through to the skin. We ran and splashed and soon I was laughing, too.

With each clomp of my boots, I felt the worry knots disintegrate, like back when I ran and threw the stick with Lucette. Down the length of my legs, through my chronically sore ankle, and out the bottoms of my feet. Then, right in front of their apartment my stoopid ankle twisted and, BOOM, I was down, wiped out on the slippery sewer grate with Diesel, heavy on top.

"*Sheise!*" she yelled.

I'd have yelled, too, but the lower half of my face was below sea level, deep in the murky waters of urban runoff. Diesel rolled over me and floundered on the curb. I tried to flip but tangled my leg in the belt from her leather jacket instead. Part of a cigarette package dripped from her forehead. Something super gross squished between my fingers. I horked loudly and tried to wipe at the grit on my face.

"Buddy! Hoo hoo, you should see yourself! Ha ha ha!" Diesel was killing herself, slapping her soggy thigh and practically peeing in utter delight.

"Look who's talking, handsome."

A piece of garbage peeled off my face and dropped into the lake of my lap, and that set Diesel off again, howling a huge Har de har har.

"Well, I'm glad I can entertain you. Try not to choke to death!" I rolled around trying to get out of the belt tangle before an oncoming car sped past, sending dirty swamp monsoon all over us again.

"Fucking Fags!"

Drunken leers in baseball caps blurred out the back window and we howled even louder, knowing that never in a million years would some people figure it out.

"Easy does it, fag." I nodded to Diesel who held open the front door of their building.

"After you, faggity fag."

"No, no. After you, Mr. Faggot Fagola."

"Fagotini," I said. "Little skinny fags."

Diesel lugged me up the steps like a fallen comrade and we burst into the brightly lit apartment. It was warm in the kitchen but not too warm, and it was clean but not too clean, and the smell of some nice, recent meal perfumed the air slightly. I didn't know what to expect but I guess not this. I stood and looked at everything and it was not like any kitchen I'd ever seen before. It was all done up in bright colors with stickers on the appliances and sexy posters of punk chicks getting it on in latex suits all over the walls. A bumper sticker on the fridge said *Vegetarians Taste Better.* A giant Cuntagion poster on the inside of the front door, when I closed it behind me, had Diesel and the band on stage, topless. I had never pictured a real kitchen where they cooked and cleaned up together, where they had a table with place settings, where they ate nice little meals, just the two of them.

"What in Joan Jett's name happened to you?!" Velvetine just stared.

"This fag here . . ." (Diesel pointed at me) ". . . fell down. And this fag here . . ." (Diesel pointed to herself) ". . . fell on top." She snorted and almost lost it again but Velvetine snapped her fingers.

"Nobody move a muscle! It's your turn to strip and all those filthy rags go right here." She kicked a plastic laundry basket our way and put the kettle on the stove. Then she plopped right down at the table and waited. She sat and *watched* us.

"No way," I said. "Cover your eyes." *Was she joking?*

"Don't drip on my floor and don't give me back talk. Come on, get cranking. Need some show music?" Velvetine pressed play on the CD player and James Brown joined us in the kitchen.

Super funkadelic.

Diesel wiggled her butt at Velvetine and slowly peeled off the mud-soaked jacket. She winked over her huge shoulder, then did a series of muscle man poses in and out of her ripped black T-shirt, growling and barking like a mad dog. I wondered if this was some weird sex game they played after a night at the bars.

"Come on, Faggy McFaggart. Rule number one: you can't say no to a lady. So, shake that money maker. Get up, get on up!"

Diesel hopped and swiveled drunkenly, deposited one article at a time with a loud SLOP! into the designated control zone. I wouldn't have called it a class act. Not exactly rivaling the Chippindales dancers or anything, but watching Diesel peel off those clothes gave me a funny feeling.

Diesel's body was a puzzle. Instead of seeming naked it was as if she had another layer under the wet clothes, one she was even more comfortable in. Each piece she took off revealed a part of the secret picture underneath. Intricate tattooed patterns around her neck trailed down the collarbones and highlighted the muscles that were really more like pecs than breasts. Her huge biceps had matching bands and the details were repeated across her clearly defined abs and again between her massive shoulder blades. Diesel snapped her Joe Boxers—men's briefs!—right at me and gave us an eyeful of buttcrack. Diesel probably had more muscles on one ass than I had on my whole body! She was like another species altogether, not male and not female. She was some courageous, beautiful mixture of the two.

"That's right, baby. Take it off!" Velvetine whistled and slipped a five-dollar bill into the waistband of Diesel's shorts. She whipped her hair around and rubbed at her face through the wet locks. When her hair fell back into place, I could see where blobs of black hair dye were staining parts of her face and neck, leaving permanent shadows on her shirt.

"Oh, oh, Velvet. Check out your make-over."

She shrieked and raced to the bathroom so I could actually remove my clothes in peace, quickly, and not looking around at anybody else.

And nobody else looking around at me.

After warm showers and while our clothes were in the washer, we drank tea and ate cinnamon toast at the kitchen table. I rubbed the knee of Diesel's clean jeans that I was wearing. I pulled at the T-shirt self-consciously. The clothes were too big for me. I felt I'd never fill them out. Never in a million years.

As we talked and joked around, I knew I was warm and safe. I hadn't felt that good in a long, long time. We looked through their photo album with page after page of Diesel's band on tour at crappy little bars filled with dykes, coast to coast.

"How's the bass coming?" she asked me.

"Well, all right." At least I could tune the thing now, and I knew all the strings. I practiced pretty much every day until my fingers were sore and my shoulders hunched with the weight of the instrument. "It's hard to not be really good at it, you know. Like I know how I want it to sound but it doesn't come out like that. Hardly ever."

"Whadja expect?" she said. "If it wasn't a fuckload of hard work, we'd all be Jimi Hendrix."

I smiled.

"G'night, Sailor. Sure you got enough sheets?" Diesel winked and ruffled my damp hair again when I nodded yes, yes for the tenth time.

"Thanks, Diesel," I said quietly. "For before."

"Anything you need, Buddy. Ever."

And off she went, down the hall, leaving me alone with my huge, overactive brain.

I lay quietly and closed my eyes but each time I did, evil flashes from Crack Mansion messed with my head. I tried to banish them. I scrinched my eyes tight and squeezed my fists straight at my sides and clenched my toes. I strained every puny muscle in my body and thought, *GO AWAY! GOTHEFUCKAWAAAY,* and the images burned right up, and then I exhaled long and loud, and away they blew. Right the fuck away.

Banished.

I don't know when I started doing that. When I was a little kid, I guess. All's I know it works. When the big, bad bogeyman creeps back in there, up in your brain, you just do the whole thing over again. You banish the shit so you have

227

some room left up there to think about other things that are nicer. I imagined things I'd like to tell Diesel.

Like, how could she tell right away I was a Buddy and not a girl she might want to date? If she was single, I mean. I wanted to tell her that sometimes I liked wearing skirts and push-up bras, and sometimes I didn't. That sometimes I didn't feel right no matter what I was wearing. I wanted to tell her that I didn't know about all that. That sometimes I wanted to be just like her, and sometimes I wanted to be with her. Someone like her who could take care of me, who knew more than me, who *had* more than me, and could afford to like me the way I was.

Those were the things I was thinking as I lay on their living room couch.

And as I drifted off to sleep I heard them whispering and sighing, laughing softly in their room, and finally just the quiet cotton music of skin rustling sheets.

chapter thirty-four

Calling Cherry

It rang and rang and rang and then it stopped. There was loud music in the background and Cherry answered in a tight, high-pitched voice.

"Cherry," I said, "It's Simone. Whatcha doin'?"

"Fuck off, ass wipe" she yelled. I heard a crash and muted yelling.

"What?"

"Not you. Talking to some asshole here. What do you want?"

She sounded speedy, her words rushed together hollow.

"You okay?"

"Huh?" she said.

"I wanted to see how you're doing. Haven't seen you in a long time, that's all."

There was a pause and I heard the shouting again and the line went static. Then it was quieter and I could tell she'd moved to a different room or something.

"Douglas, that prick, fired me, eh?"

"Yeah, I heard." When she didn't say anything, I added, "I heard you went back and threatened him with a knife. Did you? 'Coz that's what they told the cops, Cherry."

"Whateve." She exhaled. She was smoking. I could picture her. Cherry holding the phone, the other hand on hip. No, the smoke hand cutting through air to emphasize certain points, the red ember a projection of her rage.

I said, "I read your journal. What's with the Bonnie and Clyde business?"

"Me and Vincent."

"Yeah, I figured. People are saying a lot of shit about you. That you're robbing stores."

"So?"

"Well, the cops have a warrant out for you. Did you know that? They came to my place looking for you." In a rare moment of lucidity, my mom had told them to bugger off, to leave me alone, that I'd been through enough, and this had nothing to do with me. I'd hidden in the shower stall while they argued in the front hall, so I'd heard the whole thing. My mom shut the door on them, came and found me, and hugged me for a long time. It was weird, but good.

Cherry dropped the phone. There was some confusion and then she was back on the line, impatient. "Look, Simone, I gotta go."

"Where are you?" I said.

I could hear some guy talking to her, stupid Vincent probably, saying who knows what. She shushed him, and I swear I heard her say something like, "We can totally get some off her, for real." Then I had to endure Cherry, dripping honey and asking if I picked up my paycheck from last week, telling me what a great party they're going to and did I want to come, too? Oh, and that mutt missed me.

Lucette!

"Sure," I said. "I just gotta cash my paycheck first. Meet me in Punker Park tonight, okay?"

When I hung up the pay phone I smiled grimly. I had to plan the rest of my ambush.

Cherry's Blog: Most Recent Update
Friday, August 8 2:14 PM

Americans are so lucky that they can have their own guns. I love the feel of them. So hot and heavy, fucking tough. Most intense rush I had in forever. Holding it, watching the liquid fear in someone's eyes, trickle down, trickle down, piss their pants. You know you can say anything, they'll do it. They'll eat their own shit off the floor if you tell them. They'll bargain away every last appendage; dole out their limbs, their girlfriends, their children, just to save their sad fat asses.

My latest crush: 4 inch Model 10.38 special, all carbon steel, medium frame with a slightly worn blue finish. 8 7/8 inches of love in all the right places.

Mood: Laying Low, Ready to Strike
Music: Ethyl Meatplow "Queenie"

chapter thirty-five:

Ambush at Punker Park

Waiting on Cherry was nothing new. Neither was luring her places with the promise of money. I knew she'd be thrilled with my plan but Vincent would take some work. I didn't give a shit what the two of them decided to do anymore. I just wanted Lucette as far away from their madness as possible. I had dog treats in my pocket and an extra leash in the front of my hoodie. The real art would be in getting WonderDick to think it was all his idea. It would take all my self-control to not freak on the man. That's precisely why I didn't bother calling Hardcore Hank. He would've been there in a heartbeat to pound the living snot out of Vincent, or to drag Cherry off to rehab, but I couldn't picture him with a creative solution that involved flattering them into giving me what I wanted. Still, I felt optimistic. I knew in my bones it was the right thing to happen.

I was ready to trade for keeps.

I looked up at the stars and thought about going back to school in less than a month. *Impossible.* What a fucked-up summer. Carol was working, saving up, and starting university. Still in town but a world away. Carol had saved me. She cared, and once or twice even whispered the "L" word. She liked me in the boiler room and she liked me in her bedroom, but she loved me in the dark puddle of that alley, and she loved me back to life that night and lots of nights since. But she couldn't have a steady girlfriend 'coz steady girlfriends sit up late worrying while she's out working and they get jealous and make her feel bad about her job, and they get all paranoid that she actually might be getting turned on for real when she's with the clients, and then that kills the Lesbo Sex Life entirely. And then steady girlfriends treat her bad because they feel dirty inside and because deep down they also want to own a beautiful girl and when they can't it kills the romance, and next thing you know it's all over and no one invites her to the potluck suppers and she's just a man-hungry slut after all.

I wondered how many steady girlfriends Carol has had, since she knew so much about it. And me, I'd never even been to a potluck.

Carlotta was going through with her plan, to upgrade a few credits in one semester at the downtown alternative school. Pretty Boi, too. Velvetine was touring with the band and learning to play guitar. She was still gogo dancing, but also starting to make costumes for other dancers. Cherry, as we all knew, was a disaster.

I was undecided.

I leaned against a giant tree and picked at one of my piercings with its irritated swollen bump. Sooner or later Dick Wad would drive up to his usual spot and blink his headlights into the long grass and swagger out to make some deals—only this time it'd be skinny skanky Cherry who wobbled out on high heels to do lines off the hood or smoke a pipe, not all those other girls we'd ever seen with him.

I looked back up at the stars again. Still there. Twinkling. And I preferred to think of all of them way up there, doing the same thing they were doing ten minutes ago and every other night before that. Shining down through all those millions of shades of gray that kept changing, slowly, in the dying night. Each shade was probably already named and numbered for some brand of designer house paint, like Martha Stewart's billions of beiges. I stared up in the sky and imagined them all: Smokey Nights, Iron Maiden, Celtic Frost.

It was getting a bit cool. I was sore and achey from slumping on a bed of twigs and cigarette butts. I zipped up my hoodie and hugged my knees to my chest under the fabric for warmth. I lit my last smoke and wondered what fucking time it was. Carol said people smoke cigarettes when they want to be emotionally distant from someone else, like right after sex.

Of course we'd just been having sex so I put it out and smiled at her.

"Sometimes I smoke when I'm pissed off," I said.

"Better to be pissed off than pissed on," she said.

That's Carol for you.

I said, "I heard that some people make jokes when they want to be emotionally distant from someone else, like right after sex."

"Har har. At least cracking jokes doesn't give you cancer."

I tried to call up more memories of Carol and me at her apartment the other day to warm me up a bit, but I couldn't. Everything was just gray and cold and I wasn't sure what I was doing out there anymore. *Not "just gray." London Fucking Fog.*

Then the sound of a dragging muffler sat me up straight and I saw the wreck of Vincent's souped-up Honda Civic peel into the park, right where I imagined it would, and it came to a jerky halt.

For a split second there was nothing. To me it was unreality, like watching TV, which might explain why I sat there for a few minutes, not moving.

The door on the driver's side creaked open awkwardly. I could hear Cherry bitching from in there. She was trying to get out. "For fuck's sakes, help me. That mutt nearly got us killed!" She kicked the door. It swung open wider, then shut quickly against her foot. "Vincent!"

Vincent sprang out the other door and flipped the front seat forward. "Shut up. I paid a lot for this dog and she's probably ruined now."

"I paid a lot for these shoes and they're probably ruined," she whined.

Cherry struggled out of the car, her arms full of blanket. She set it on the grass near the car. Vincent carried Lucette. He walked away, set her under a nearby tree. He tapped at her with his shoe a few times and threw his hands up in the air.

No!

"How could you not see her?! Huh? You drive like a fucking maniac, you know that, bitch?" He paced back and forth, pulling at his hair.

"I never said I knew how to drive. That wasn't the plan. And the dog was supposed to be in the car, not out pissing on the back tire, or whatever it was doing. You're lucky I even got us out of the parking lot." Cherry looked pretty messed up. She tripped over to Vincent and rubbed his shoulders.

"Don't! Just don't touch me right now, okay?"

"Come on, Vincent. Chill. It's all good. We got the money. Skanktank the Moron is paid off, so the rest is ours. Come on, it was a blast!" She hopped onto the hood of the car and lit a joint. "Here. Smoke this."

He did and I guess it helped because he sat down beside her and they finished it in silence.

They didn't even notice me, curled up behind the big tree, peering around the trunk at them. Lucette didn't move at all.

But the blanket did.

The blanket shimmied and there was some wriggling and a muffled sound. It fell over and started to unroll. It was a goddamn baby. A little kid. The crying got louder.

"Shit. I almost forgot about it." Cherry looked over, disinterested.

"What the fuck do we do with that?" Vincent spat on the grass.

Cherry said, "I can't believe the little fucker pissed on my new jeans."

"So?"

"We should probably take off. I don't see Simone, the traitor. Hey! Why don't we keep the baby?" said Cherry. "We'll be like a little family."

"Yeah?"

"Yeah. Kiss me, stupid."

"Don't call me stupid. I fucking HATE that. Never never call me that again. Got that, bitch?"

"I was only joking, stu— . . . come on . . . Kiss." Cherry straddled his legs and roped her arms around his neck.

That's when I finally stood up. It'd only been a couple of minutes but everything seemed slow motion to me, ever since I'd seen Lucette. I walked quietly, in my trancey dream state again. I couldn't make sense of this situation, it was so far from anything I'd imagined. The baby was making quite a racket. When he saw me he raised his little arms in the air to be picked up. His face was covered in snot and tears. A regular crybaby mess. And he looked like Carlotta's baby cousin, only terrified and dirty.

"Shhh, shhh. Hey there." I lifted him up, wet pants and all. One of his shoes was missing. That's when I recognized the hand made socks. *Impossible!*

"What the fuck are you doing?" said Vincent.

Cherry swiveled around and almost lost her balance. "Heyyy, Simone."

"Cherry, why is Pablo here?"

"No, that's Vincent. You know."

"I mean the baby. What are you doing with him?"

"It's ours now. Right, Vincent?" Cherry smiled crookedly up at him.

He said, "That's our hostage, eh? From the Wal-Mart raid." Vincent pointed at me. "So put him down."

"You shoulda seen it, Simone. I fucking rocked the house!" She mimed it out for me, mock fear, hands up, knees quaking, fake blubbering.

I was hot with rage. A regular goddamn bonfire.

"Fuck you, Cherry. You too, Vincent. You guys are sick."

"Who you talking to, ya fuckin' dyke?" Vincent slid off the car and stepped towards me.

"This is Carlotta's nephew!" I screamed. "Where did you get him? You could've killed him."

"Maybe the stoopid bitch shouldn't take her kid to work," said Cherry. "We didn't know he was under the cash, okay? Everything happened so fast." Then after a pause she said, "Small fuckin' world, eh?"

I stormed past them, carrying Pablito. I headed over to Lucette, lying in a heap by that other tree. "What did you do to her? Is she even alive?" I was shrieking. Hysterical, really, and vibrating with adrenaline. "What is wrong with you two?!"

"Come on, Vincent. Let's get out of here. I'm sick, all right. Sick of hearing this crap."

"You think I wanted MY DOG hit by this fucking car?! Is that what you're saying?" Vincent lunged towards me. His eyes were crazy mean. "Is that what you're saying, bitch dyke? That's *my* fucking dog, not yours. She's ruined. Think that makes me happy? Do ya?!" He took a swing at me but was too far away. His fist flew through the air, useless.

"You think he's all that, Cherry, but he's just another Frank. And you're so screwed up you're giving it away free. Better watch your back. He sure as hell won't."

I kept walking, switched Pablo around on my hip so it wasn't so hard to hold him.

I heard a loud click.

"No, you watch your back. Stop right there."

I did, because I knew that sound down to my knees. I turned slowly and smoothly to face the revolver, held tightly in Cherry's twitchy hands.

chapter thirty-six

Resistance is Fertile

Cherry shivered in her tiny T-shirt. She paced back and forth arguing with Vincent. Neither of them made any sense. I was embarrassed for them, frankly. Fighting over cigarettes at a time like this. They had a bag of money in the car. They could've bought as many cartons as they wanted. Christ, they had a gun! They could've robbed every corner store for miles.

I was cold and sore and my ass hurt from sitting on the bench for so long, holding Pablito. I watched Lucette, too. She was breathing steadily now. She hadn't moved much but Vincent had let me put a blanket from the car on top of her, and wipe the goop out of her eyes. Her gums were gray. She was in shock. I'd taken a corner of the blanket, dipped it in water I brought over from the fountain in a dirty, dented Frisbee, and squeezed drops into her mouth. She'd blinked at me and did a little lick of the water drops, and I'd felt hopeful.

Vincent was yelling some bullshit and then, totally mid-sentence, just blanked. He had no clue what he was on about.

"Whaa?" He stood there, mouth hanging open a bit. He yawned.

Cherry blinked and sniffed.

This is your brain on drugs.

"Hey," I said. "Shouldn't you be planning your big get-away?"

"Shut up, Simone," she snapped.

"No, she's right. We should probably take off," said Vincent.

He lurched over to the car and opened the driver's side.

"Aren't you going to change cars?" I smiled helpfully.

"Shut UP!" yelled Cherry.

Vincent looked from her to me and back again. "Well, I could borrow my cousin's." He scratched his head.

"Well, I'm not walking over there. You come and pick me up," she said.

I rolled my eyes.

Homicidal slapstick.

I rocked Pablo slowly while their voices crashed in crescendo. I tried to become invisible when Vincent screamed frustration right in Cherry's face. He grabbed his leather jacket and a black gym bag from the back seat. He stormed back over to Cherry, took the cigarette out of her mouth and kissed her. Then he turned, strode out towards the street, and flicked the butt over his shoulder. He never once looked back.

Cherry stood, wavering and forlorn, watching Vincent disappear. The dark circles under her eyes made her look old, forsaken, like she was about to crash. It was her worst time of day. *Evil tide.*

Personally, I could've kissed him goodbye, too. I was convinced I could manage Cherry without him, even if she still had the gun. I stretched my legs. Stood up slowly.

"Wait. You're not going anywhere!"

"I want to check Lucette again, Cherry. Come on!"

"Nice try." Cherry was sooo paranoid. She was a jumpy, wired mess.

"Cherry, I'm not going anywhere, for fuck's sake." She jerked her head in Lucette's direction and I moved over, taking Pablito with me. Stretched out long and quiet, Lucette looked like a baby bear. Big black nose, pokey teeth and that long tongue lolling out onto the grass. Deep brown eyes. Like chocolate. I fed her some more water drops and this time she met me partway, sucked the flannel nipple with the tip of her mouth. Her paws lay limp and the pushy pads on the bottom were dry and cracked. I stroked the furry tops lightly. She blinked.

For once there were no kids sleeping nearby, no hobos parked under any bushes that I could see. I wished for some health nut to jog by on an early morning run. Or those old people, come to do some Tai Chi. They could rescue us. I figured the real tragedy in modern life wasn't that there were no heroes left, like some people say, but more like all those potential heroes were just stuck in traffic, or sitting on the can when you needed them. Just in the wrong time and place to do their thing. That, I believed, was the petty truth. It made me chuckle a little sardonic laugh.

"What's so funny?" Cherry glared at me.

"Nothing," I said. "Just thinking."

"Well, cut it the fuck out. Back on the bench. I'm the one who needs to think."

No kidding.

I went back and sat down. The only phone booth was on the other side of the Punker Park. Without the kid I could outrun Cherry. Could I outrace her gun?

Pablito slept. This was the longest I'd ever held him. Normally, at Carlotta's place, someone was always reaching for him, patting, smoothing, playing with him. You'd have him for a bit but another set of hands would be ready to take him. He had a deep frown on his little face. Dimpled chin. Dark lashes. Every now and then he made little baby breathing noises that helped me focus. I sent him all the body heat I could spare. I said all kinds of nice baby things in my mind and sent the pictures down my arms and out through my fingers into the dirty bundle that was him. It was kind of like talking, only without your mouth.

When Cherry wasn't looking, I pulled the blanket corners behind me, over one shoulder, and wound them tightly around to the front. I tried to do it the way Carlotta's aunt wrapped him up with her brightly colored shawls. She attached him to her front by tying the cloth around her waist somehow. I couldn't quite make the knot.

"You know, this kid's gonna be really hungry when he wakes up. He'll probably start screaming. You should take off before all that happens, don't you think?"

"Right now he's our hostage and you're nothing but the babysitter, so shut up and shut him the fuck up. I'm not leaving 'til Vincent gets back." Cherry chewed her thumbnail down to the quick.

I was incredulous. "You really think he's coming back for you?"

I stretched the blanket tighter and tried again to secure it. *Almost got it.*

"Of course. He's clearing out some shit, packing up his cousin's car. We're going away."

"You sure about that?"

Infiltrate with doubt.

"Shut up!" She waved the gun at me again.

I talked softly and slowly. I bit back my fear of her. It sat in my gut like poison. "I know you've got a gun, all right? And a crappy car that the cops are looking for, and a really hurt dog, and a kidnapped baby. Where's the money, Cherry? Vincent took it, didn't he?"

She was listening. At least I thought so. I hoped all my talk was eating away at her. I stopped being able to read her ages ago, before the summer even started and stuff got wacked right out of control.

"Cherry," I said. "Lucette needs a vet. Now. This baby needs to go home. And I have to take a piss. Take off while you still can."

I yanked on that chewed-up blanket end and tried again. *Got it!* I shifted myself, carefully leaned forward. I tested that it would hold Pablo's weight in case I needed my hands for other things. Cherry lowered the gun and looked out past the edge of the park, to the street that Vincent had taken, where every few minutes people drove past in their nice cars, oblivious to our little urban drama. It amazed me to think we were still right there, hidden amongst the trees.

"What would you do if you were him?" I said. "I mean, really. It's probably nothing personal."

Cherry winced when I said that and her face slackened. She knew it was true. Worse, she was the one who had sent him away. If it had been her, she'd have been miles away by now, tossing back the Jack Daniels and cranking up a jukebox. She didn't say a word but turned abruptly and headed to the car. She crawled in and started rifling through all the crap in there. Her bony ass jutted out from the driver's side. She tossed stuff onto the grass behind her. I didn't know what she was looking for but I didn't wait to find out.

I ran.

My legs were cold and stiff from no circulation. They were clumsy chunks of wood and the ankles felt painfully rigid, but they worked. I chanted to myself, *MoveMoveMove,* and pumped my right arm up and down for momentum. The left supported Pablo against my chest. He was heavier by the second, a million pounds by now, and the phone was farther than I thought. *Run, Forrest, Run!* I stared at the phone. I was getting there. I was pounding across the grass. Pablo's head banged against me, woke him. He was sucking back some big air, and his whole little body was tensing up for a giant wail, and I couldn't breathe—and then I heard it behind me.

Not a gunshot. Not a scream. The muffler backfired and the engine whined.

She was driving the car through the park, chasing us down to kill us both.

The gears shifted horribly.

For a second I thought I'd actually make it to the phone. I imagined maybe the car would stall, or that Tai Chi troupe would spring out from behind a recycling box after all, or some other Hollywood miracle would conspire to deliver us from evil. That's probably when I snuck a peak over my shoulder and caught my stiff boot on the tree root. It was definitely when I felt myself reeling forward, out of control, and I was falling, falling, face down.

I heard the car lurch forward. Pablo screamed in terror. I put my right hand out to break the impact, twisted to avoid crushing him. I landed heavy, hard, on my right shoulder, squeezed the hell out of Pablo. My head banged on the ground. I scrabbled in the dirt, dragged us around the big tree trunk as the car crashed through the underbrush and into the small clearing. It was an instant of chaos and I realized with a shock that it was me making those animal noises, screaming at her, at the car, at everything.

The car slammed hard into the giant tree trunk, the same one I'd hidden behind earlier that night, and a sickening crunch of metal told me it had stopped. There was silence. Only the echo of that ungodly thud and then a staggered ticking from inside the crumpled hood of the car. Pain surged through my shoulder and the whole of my right side. I crawled away from the tree. I pulled myself and the tangled blanket with Pablo, somehow still inside there, away away and over to the phone. The racket had raised more than a fuss. It already had neighbors looking out their windows, sniffing the air for trouble.

Who the fuck did I think I was going to call? Surely not the pigs.

I even had a quarter, although it was really hard to get at it, to hold it still, to put it neatly in the proper slot, the way I was shaking. Dialing was practically impossible.

After, I walked the other way. Past the tree where people were starting to gather. Past the smashed-up car. Away from the sirens that grew louder. Over to where Lucette was. She'd tried to get away and managed a few feet. She was under a bush, hiding from all those scary sounds. Pablo and I found a quiet spot to wait.

Our heroes were all on their way.

chapter thirty-seven:
Rescue Squad

"You should probably split, Buddy, in case anyone recognizes you." Diesel paced back and forth beside her motorcycle. She lit another cigarette. "Jesus. What a mess."

More sirens panicked their way across the city. We were hiding away from the ruckus, as far as we could without deserting Lucette. I tried to pass Pablo over. He was leaking from both ends.

"Oh, no. I can't hold a baby. What am I gonna do with that? It's crying. I'll probably break it or something."

I sat down again and held Pablo in my left arm. He weighed a billion pounds.

Diesel said, "I called the emergency vet clinic from home. They don't usually do pickups but they don't usually have to deal with me, right? I'll stay with your dog, there. Okay?"

"Thanks."

She exhaled smoke and squinted at me. "Why dincha tell me what was going on, Buddy?"

Diesel was solid. Solid with a teeny, wavering nerve I'd never seen before. I never imagined she felt fear, which was pretty stupid of me, I guess, but tiny rays of it were shining in her eyes now. She was scared of what had gone down out there and I was pretty sure she was a little scared of me. Of the messes I'd been getting into, of all those things I hadn't told her. She had thought she knew all about me and my teen dyke angst, but no. Not even.

"Did you see her?" I knew Diesel would tell it straight up. No candy coating.

"On a stretcher. They took her in an ambulance. I got here just as they were leaving. I'll stop by the hospital as soon as Lucette's settled up. Okay?" Diesel ran her hands through her short hair. "Some crazy shit. I heard some cops talking about her boyfriend. He got arrested a couple blocks away. Dude's fucked 'coz he started whaling on one of them."

"Good," I said venomously. No love lost for either party.

She unclipped her apartment keys from the rest of them on the ring. "You can make it back to our place, right? Hank's coming to pick you up."

"It's okay, Diesel," I said. "I want to take Pablito home, first."

Diesel looked at me closely. "You sure?"

"Yeah, man. Thanks a lot, though. You were the first person I thought of. To call, I mean." I smiled.

Diesel smiled, too. It was a sad one, a tired one, but it was all right. She said, "Well, look who's here."

More quietly she said, "Buddy, you owe me big time. Chicks love to take care of bruised-up heroes. So I guess it's your lucky day."

Carol slammed her cab door and ran across the grass towards us.

Carol!

"You called her?" I couldn't imagine having Carol witness another of my devastating dramas.

"Velvetine did."

Carol came up to me, right up to my face, and kissed me. She was wearing a pink hoodie and her sexy cutoffs. Her hair was strangled back in a puffy ponytail and she wasn't wearing any makeup.

"I came as soon as I could," she said. She took Pablito from me, and did a quick inspection. He was smelly, dirty, wet, and loud. Carol jiggled him and swung him gently side to side against her hip. She wiped snot from his nose, wiped his face, smiled at him. He stopped crying, sensing that she was a more proficient caretaker. He seemed intrigued by her fruity smelling hair and gorgeous smile.

Who wasn't?

A rattling muffler coughed through loud music (the BFG's!), and Hardcore Hank's rusted, piece-of-shit van pulled into view. Diesel pushed me gently in that direction.

Carol said, "Hey, I'm coming with you."

A deep voice called out, "Hey Freaks. Hardcore Hank, at your cervix."

"Hey," I said to him. "Whatcha doing here?"

"Giving you ladies a ride." He winked lewdly. "Who's first?"

"Ha ha . . . me," said Carol. She climbed into the front with the baby.

I dragged my sorry ass into the back, next to all the crap he kept in there. A lumpy single mattress where he sometimes slept, depending. Cans of motor oil and dirty rags and empty beer cans, crushed and leaking the perfume of stale and rancid ale.

"Hank," I said, "Some love palace. Is this a porno mag back here?" I peered at the glossy pages and figured as much, but it was hard to tell what with the huge oil spill on the cover.

"Yeah, wanna borrow it?" He grinned at me in the rearview mirror. "Where we headed?"

And so we drove Pablo home. Home to Nestor and Jorge, who swore they'd kill Vincent if he wasn't already dead or locked up by noon the next day. Home to Isabelle and 'Lisabeth, who hugged Pablo and wiped their faces and then went to pour him a bath. Home to Carlotta and her desperate aunt, who'd been up all night weeping. After the robbery, she'd taken off, first on foot and then in a taxi, trying to chase down Cherry and Vincent in their car. She was a changed woman when she finally arrived home, empty-handed. Now she held him and fed him, inspected every scrape. Home to Carlotta's mom, a beautiful and remarkable woman who had survived all manner of atrocity before escaping to Canada. When she opened the door and first saw him in Carol's arms, those deeply etched grief lines softened a bit. Carlotta's mom pulled us in and hugged me hard against her, squeezed my sore arm tight, looked into my eyes deeply. Two obsidian pools. She said, "Thank you," in her quiet and dignified manner. There was nothing else to say, really.

After a bit, it was time for us to leave. They needed to be alone, just their *familia*. Besides, Hardcore Hank was making them a bit nervous. Not intentionally, or anything. He was just a bit louder and dirtier and more reckless than they were used to. I wanted to go home, to be quiet, and to sit by my mom, even if it wouldn't be like on TV where the mothers usually say and do the right things and make the kid feel safe again, at the end of the show. Hank dropped Carol off at her place first. She kissed and kissed me goodbye, out there on the curb. We wanted to kiss some more but Hank honked and pretended to be wanking through the window, so I hopped back in, this time in the front seat.

Then he drove me to my place, right up to the door.

chapter thirty-eight

Bail Court

"Empty your pockets, put all items in the tray, and walk slowly through the metal detector, please." The security guard was a bosomy woman in a tight blue uniform. Her male counterpart stood glaring at me, hands hanging loosely at his side.

I dumped out crap. People behind me got restless, coughed loudly. I guess they knew what to do and were all ready to zip through in their turn. But I had a lot of pockets in those army pants and it was hard to clear them out one-handed. Righty was in a sling and lefty was new on the job. A wrinkled five-dollar bill, half a stick of gum, a broken cigarette, a folded fortune from some long ago cookie, one subway token, pocket fluff. Thank God I didn't have any weed on me. I was clearing out my jean jacket when she blew her whistle, right in my face.

"Knife!" She yelled and her eyes bugged out crazily.

The guy was on me like sunscreen, holding my wrist hard, spinning me, pushing me face down on the metal table. Hot pain seared through my right side. The camping knife and my lighter went flying.

"Ow," I yelled. "Jeez."

When the guy got off me I thanked him. "You're all man," I said straight-faced, and, "Thanks for relocating my shoulder."

Relocating where, we don't know.

So I guess you're not supposed to have any weapons when you go into court. Ironically enough, they wouldn't hold it for me, they couldn't keep it anywhere even though they both felt a bit bad about the whole takedown thing. I had to stash my knife at the bottom of a garbage can in the same hallway. Then I waltzed back up to the security entrance for a second go at it.

"Here I come," I called out slowly. "Easy now, no tackling this time."

Smooth sailing.

I sat on a wooden bench in bail court for hours. I witnessed bleary-eyed, wild-haired men in orange jumpsuits sit and scratch and stare into the courtroom, handcuffed one to the next, as the judge worked his way down the long list of names. I heard one wacked story after another as the strange details of their alleged crimes were read aloud from computer printouts by lawyers and his highness, The Judge.

Fascinating.

Finally they brought him in. Orange was definitely not his color. Vincent was a skanky, wired mess, and it looked like someone had roughed him up pretty recently.

If only Cherry could see him now.

I moved to the front row and stared until he made eye contact with me. He half smiled at me, eyebrow cocked hopeful, and I realized he thought I was there to post his bail. I stared back evenly. I scratched the side of my nose slowly, with my middle finger. It was immature, I know, but satisfying. That's when he figured out I wasn't there to help him. He narrowed his eyes. I widened my smile. He stood up, glaring, he leaned forward. He hissed at me, ignoring the judge who told him to sit down, ignoring the ramblings of someone else's lawyer pleading a stranger's case.

I laughed. I laughed out loud and Vincent lost it. He started yelling. A vein pulsed in his neck. He lunged forward, pulling the men's arms on either side of him. It looked like he was going to hurdle the wooden box they were sitting in.

"I'll fucking kill you, you stupid bitch," he screamed.

Prison guards were on him in a flash. One held him around the neck from behind. Vincent's face was red, almost purple. The Judge banged the gavel and called "Order! Order!" He threatened to kick me out for disrupting his court.

"I'm leaving," I said in a loud, clear voice. I stood up stiffly. "Just wanted you to know I'm keeping the dog."

Vincent gurgled some more venom before the guards unlocked him from the lineup and dragged him out the little back door.

Five big guards for one little creep.

I limped my way out of the room, down the hall, past my friends at security, and over to the garbage to retrieve my knife. Then I booked it the hell out of there. I was heading home.

Cherry's Blog: Most Recent Update
Friday August 22 3:23 PM

Dear World with a Pulse:

I am alive. Barely. What's left of me is locked up, detoxing, stir-crazy, and celibate. More or less. I am only allowed twenty minutes on this lousy computer. We have a curfew, bunk beds, disgusting food, tough bitches. Just like in the movies! So, part of my Juvie Rehab penance is I'm supposed to apologize to everyone I fucked over. Mainly I guess that'd be Simone. Of the people I know personally, that is. Here goes.

Dear Simone: I'm sorry I tried to run you over with the car that day in the park. I didn't really mean it. I was tripping. It seemed smart at the time, but I just ended up busting my leg, totaling the car and getting sent to Detox Mountain, the amusement park for twisted young female offenders. I don't suppose you'll ever forgive me just as long as you know that I think what I did totally sucked. Not just with the car, either. You were my best friend and I treated you like shit. I miss our old times. I know you won't, but I wish you could visit.

Speaking of which,

Dear Carlotta: It's been great catching up with you, especially since we weren't that tight before the big blow out, but for fuck's sakes! I only get one visitor a week and if you keep charging up here every Monday morning at the crack of dawn, I'll never see anyone else. Not that my mom is racing over or anything. And Vincent is gone for a couple years, I guess. Talk about a long-distance love affair. His spelling's atrocious, by the way. You know I'm sorry about the whole baby fiasco. The kidnapping thing. Peace out.

The Giant Cyborg Security Guard says my time is up and the Earnest Fruity Social Worker wants me to join them In Group. I'd rather eat nails. Only seventeen and a half months to go.

Love, Cherry.

chapter thirty-nine

Mosh Pit Revisited

The line moved up. We were almost at the front. I made a show of getting out my fake ID, courtesy of Hardcore Hank. The bouncers scanned documents ahead of us. They were giving some girl a hard time. She and her pubescent friend got the boot and the older guys they were with made lame apologies but slid on through, into the bar and the smoke and the noise without them. The door slammed shut and we were up.

Carlotta smiled and said we were on the guest list. CroMagnum lowered his heavy lids and I purred, "Hey, Hi" to him and he elbowed his buddy, the new guy, and said, "They're cool."

"Wasn't it your friend's birthday a while back?" He licked his lips.

I tilted my head and said, "You remembered? That's so sweet."

"Haven't seen you girls around for a while."

"Been busy."

Pretty Boi laughed and said, "She shore has, mister."

Carlotta shoved Pretty Boi all playful like and gave the doorguys some sexy attitude and then—*Voilà!*—the door opened and we were in. Sure enough, we were on the list, so we got in free, no hassles. First, we headed for the bar. You always buy the first drink so they know you have money and also so you have a cup to refill from your flask. Diesel was over by the stage and Hatchet was double-checking their gear on stage. Choosy Soozy was drinking shots at the bar with her friends. I cheersed her with my fist because I didn't have a beer yet, and she yelled, "Hey, thanks for coming to the show!"

Like we were doing her a personal favor or something.

Soozy yelled over to me could I give her a hand? And I said, "Sure." She meant literally. She was tightening the side laces of her leather pants and asked me to hold the knot with my finger when she did the final tie. When she was done pulling, my finger was still in there, tight against her thigh. Near her hip.

Halfway between her ass and her crotch!

"Hey," I said.

My finger was losing circulation fast. It was starting to hurt. I didn't want to let on that there was a problem, but nobody seemed to realize I was attached to her pants. I was thinking *Oh fuck!* and trying to wriggle it loose, but nope, it wasn't working. I looked around madly. Carlotta and Pretty Boi were kissing. Soozy was talking to her friends, but any second now she would rear up and jog over to the stage and there I'd be, dragging along after her, hanging from her Ass! I tugged harder with the paralyzed hand. Then I said (quietly so as not to embarrass anyone), "Hey, man."

Soozy said, "You calling me a man?"

"No," I stammered. "No, you're definitely one hundred percent all womanly."

"That why you got your hand all up in my pants?" she said.

I said, "Ohmygod."

Then the bartender said, "Never mind, sweetie. Soozy's always trying to take someone home with her. Usually she waits 'til last call for the finger hold." And then she smiled and I realized they were teasing me. *Possibly flirting!*

Soozy laughed but not mean, like, and said, "Want your finger back yet?"

I nodded and she said, "You're Diesel's friend, right?"

And I felt like I might bust in two. "I'm Simone."

"Well, Simone, you're a pretty good sport." She released my finger and double-knotted the leather lacing without my skin in there.

"This is Carlotta," I gestured, "and that's Pretty Boi."

Soozy shook their hands and adjusted her orange push-up bra. Snatch and Hatchet and Diesel and Velvetine came over and joined us for a beer. The place was really filling up by then, and the gals were getting hyper, pre-show nerves.

"Hey, you left so early the other day," said Velvetine. She was fixing her pink and silver bouffant wig.

"Yeah," I said. "Thanks again for letting me crash. I had fun."

"Us too, Buddy." Diesel pretended to head-butt me. "You missed an awesome breakfast, though. Next time no quick exits. Velvetine makes a mean tofu sausage and my pancakes rock!"

I smiled but inside I was suddenly sad, remembering the last time I ate pancakes. In the diner, with Cherry. She was bummed because Vincent had stood her up again. He was busy breaking in some other chick. Humiliation stained her face, plain as pie. In one beautiful, lucid moment she'd looked at me and said, "When the fuck did I start paying for a two-bit lay?" I'd nearly choked—it had surprised the hell out of me. She tapped the table with conviction and declared the whole summer a waste. "You think I don't know what's going on," she said, quietly. "But I do. I'm way ahead of you, Simone, so don't think I'm getting played or I need to be rescued. I picked this, somehow. I know it."

Diesel popped me one on the shoulder, snapped me back to reality. The gals were filing backstage to get the rest of their gear. Pretty Boi and Carlotta waltzed over and double hugged me.

"You having fun, *Carnala*?" Carlotta was a little bit drunk. I could tell because her long arms hung loose and she was smiling indiscriminately.

Pretty Boi laughed and rubbed my head. Then the guitars ripped into the air and there was no talking anymore 'coz it was too fucking loud. Velvetine stomped on stage with an electric drummel and proceeded to attack her cybersonic lingerie, sending a steady stream of sparks into the audience from the front of her metallic thong. The crowd loved it.

Who wouldn't? I mean, really.

Carlotta, Pretty Boi, and I joined the rush. We banged around down in front, fixated by the stage show like everybody else, but also swept up by the music and partying in the pit. Just once I thought I saw the ghost of Cherry, slamming beside me, and it freaked me right out. Hank appeared, and we bopped around until he spilled too much beer, as per usual. Off he staggered, into the steamy crowd.

After the first set, Carlotta, Pretty Boi, and I all plopped down in a pile.

"Too bad you have to work tonight," said Pretty Boi. He pulled the bottom part of his *Somebody shoot the President* T-shirt up through the collar and back down on the inside of his shirt.

"Now you have a bikini," I said.

You could see his six pack and the Gothic lettering that started somewhere on his smooth chest and traveled over those abs, below his navel, and lead down, down into the mysteries of his faded blue jeans.

I hated the thought of jetting right when the party was going strong. All the way over to that godforsaken concrete room. Last time there weren't any extra girls to fill in for You-Know-Who so I had to flop and roll around on the floor all by my lonely. The Boys wanted me to do a full on Solo Jerk Off scene, but I said twelve bucks an hour wasn't enough. There it was, my first labor dispute in the porn industry.

"What time is it anyway?"

Carlotta steamrolled me, completely out of character, and stuck her wristwatch in my face. "Eleven-twenty," she announced.

"Simone, you're late!" Pretty Boi looked shocked.

I pulled myself up and saluted them. "Fuck the Web site! I'm staying here!"

They whistled and cheered. Then we bought more beer.

"Too bad Carol's not here," said Pretty Boi, later at the bar.

"Yeah," I agreed. "But it'll be great to meet her for breakfast in a couple hours."

"Stud!" he shrieked and hugged me tight.

chapter forty

Into the Sunset

We stepped out from the air conditioned coolness of the Animal Hospital, fearsome, into the bright sunlight. People stared. Until I looked back at them, full in the face, and they twitched away unnaturally. Their eyes darted. Didn't like being caught in the act. If Cherry had been here, she would have shot them the finger. Maybe yelled some obscenities. But I didn't blame them. Those Jealous Fuckers that couldn't stop staring were maybe wishing they had our life, and not their own.

Carlotta looked fantastic, for one thing. Two thick black braids hung on either side of her beautiful face. Huge, black eyes framed by high cheekbones were balanced by a luscious set of lips. She absolutely demanded reactions from strangers, driving by in their cars, shuffling towards us on the sidewalk, and zipping past on bikes. Carlotta was strutting along in her open-toed platform shoes, bright red miniskirt, and tiny, ripped *Nobody Knows I'm Transsexual!* T-shirt. She held Pablo on her hip and he snuggled against her warm skin, moved tiny fists along the edge of her top, made little baby sounds.

Next to Carlotta I looked pretty rough, but it had been a bad summer for me and getting knocked around, so whateve'. My big boots needed a polish. My cutoffs hung low with the extra weight of my heavy metal belt buckle, and the chain that clipped onto my wallet. I was wearing Pretty Boi's *New York Dolls* shirt. I was feeling perky in spite of my wounds 'coz I had a fresh shave and new colors. Deep greens and blues mixed around in there with black near the roots. Underwater Sea Queen with one Band-Aid in my usual spot.

Lucette sauntered along on her new leash. She had a new thick collar with four rows of silver studs scaring the pants off your average citizen. She was doing pretty well, all things considered. One paw was bandaged up so she had a distinguished limp going on. Her back hip was still hurting and her ribs were tender.

Whose weren't?

For the first time since I was a little kid I was actually looking forward to the fall, to starting at this new school downtown that Carlotta had discovered. I wanted to be able to let myself go. Not in a drifting kind of way, but in a relaxed and focused way, like how it felt practicing my bass. It was hard work but it was good to move through something new and be changed by it. To become different.

To become.

Carlotta broke into my thoughts. "What you gonna do with Lucette? Your girl Cherry says you *tiefed* her from Vincent. She says he paid good money for her and she's still a puppy, like five months or something."

"Vincent left her to die," I said. "That fucker's in jail so he just better try to come and get her. And Cherry never liked Lucette, so I don't see how it's any of her business."

She said, "*Gringa* sure is bored up there. Think you'll visit her?"

"Nope. Not for a long time, Carlotta. Maybe never."

She nodded.

Everything was still too fresh. I was working through some ugly and surprising realizations, that it wasn't all poor me, woe is me. I had lived off the sparks that Cherry generated, lapped them up greedily, and complained only when they burnt me more than I liked or in ways I hadn't imagined. I made her my proxy then felt betrayed when she veered off on a course that excluded me. I dug in my nails and teeth, tried to keep parts of her for myself, clearly against her will. That Cherry was finally gone from me forever was clear. The idea that I had somehow played a part in all this was new and it gnawed at me, quietly insistent.

I stroked Lucette's head and her softsoft ears. "I don't see how we'd ever put up with that shite again, anyhow. Right?"

Lucette barked, "Fuck Yeah," and licked my hand. Then she left her mouth open so the tongue dripped out a bit and her brown eyes twinkled up at us—well, at me, really—and her wee, stumpy tail whipped back and forth. I knew it was just something dogs did, but it looked to me like she was smiling and that just killed me. Knocked me right out. We admired the way the sun was burning its way west with us, sinking below the rooftops and pulling out the stops with some fiery magic. *Tropical lipsticks.* We were passing Punker Park. I shuddered but hardly even looked over there at all that memory madness. The torn up tire tracks that scarred the lawn. The terrible mark at the base of the big tree.

We just kept walking. We knew a better park with lots more space. Way more trees and bushes and flowery things. Where you can run off leash for as long as you want.